The Last Novel

By
David Markson

16

EasyRead Large

Copyright Page from the Original Book

Library of Congress Cataloging-in-Publication Data

Markson, David.
 The last novel / David Markson.
          p. cm.
 ISBN-13: 978-1-59376-143-1
 ISBN-10: 1-59376-143-0
1. Novelists—Fiction. 2. Fiction—Authorship—Fiction.
3. Psychological fiction. I. Title.

PS3563.A67L37 2007
813'.54—dc22   2006038793

Cover design by Kimberly Glyder Design
Interior design by David Bullen
Printed in the United States of America

 Shoemaker & Hoard
www.shoemakerhoard.com

10 9 8 7 6 5 4 3 2 1

RHYW

ReadHowYouWant partners with publishers to provide books for ALL Kinds of Readers. For more information about Becoming A (RHYW) Registered Reader and to find more titles in your preferred format, visit:
www.readhowyouwant.com

PRAISE FOR DAVID MARKSON

VANISHING POINT

"Breathtakingly seamless perfection ... brilliant, high, fine, masterful, deep."

Kirkus Reviews (starred review)

"Striking, devilishly playful ... and with a deeply philosophical core, this novel proves once more that Markson deserves his accolades and then some."

Publishers Weekly (starred review)

"David Markson's books are stunningly true and wildly inventive. They are unsettling and consoling. They are full of strange echoes, paradoxes, and hilarious stories, and in their accumulations they are great homages to great art, celebrating the work of the imagination and at the same time reminding us of swift time and the fragility of cultural memory."

Joanna Scott

"Irresistible ... a marvelous, page-turning read ... uncommon brilliance ... a novel of immense drama ... explosively artful."

Baltimore Sun

THIS IS NOT A NOVEL

"Magnificent ... it's almost impossible to stop turning pages ... my soul was humming."

Sven Birkerts, *New York Observer*

"Reads as addictively as an airport thriller ... masterful."

Bookforum

"Mesmerizing."

Newsday

"Triumphant ... plangent verbal music ... altogether wonderful."

Michael Dirda, *Washington Post Book World*

"No, it's not a novel, but it is a masterwork."

Publishers Weekly

READER'S BLOCK

"Alarmingly moving ... yes, you should read this book."

Believer

"No one but Beckett can be quite as sad and funny at the same time as Markson can."

Ann Beattie

"One of the most original novels of its time ... unputdownable."

American Book Review

WITTGENSTEIN'S MISTRESS

"Addresses formidable philosophic questions with tremendous wit. Remarkable."

Amy Hempel, *New York Times Book Review*

"A work of genius ... An erudite, breathtakingly cerebral novel whose prose is crystal and whose voice rivets and whose conclusion defies you not to cry."

David Foster Wallace, *Review of Contemporary Fiction*

"Provocative, learned, wacko, brilliant, and extravagantly comic."

William Kennedy

"The novel I liked best this year ... one dizzying, delightful, funny passage after another."

Washington Times

SPRINGER'S PROGRESS

"An exuberantly Joycean, yes, Joycean celebration of carnality and creativity—an everything-goes, risk-taking, manically wild and funny and painful novel ... brilliant."

New York Times Book Review

"Alive with the pleasures of language ... terribly funny, formidably intelligent."

Jonathan Yardley, *Washington Post*

"The most honest and stunning Greenwich Village novel of my time."

Seymour Krim

GOING DOWN

"Beautifully constructed. One of the most important books published in America in years."

Frederick Exley

"A beauty. A haunting story of passion and flesh. An erotic work of art."

William Goyen

"A book we will come back to as we do with *The Recognitions* and *Under the Volcano.* An unquestioned masterpiece."

Les Whitten

"Leaves me woozy with sex and death and Mexico. Highly recommended."

Kurt Vonnegut

"A contemporary, very literate record of despair; all of it in fact seems to be taking place in darkness, in shadows, in the rain, or in the secret criminal places of the heart ... supremely successful."

Village Voice

Also by David Markson

NOVELS

The Ballad of Dingus Magee
Going Down
Springer's Progress
Wittgenstein's Mistress
Reader's Block
This Is Not a Novel
Vanishing Point

CRITICISM

Malcolm Lowry's Volcano: Myth, Symbol, Meaning

POETRY

Collected Poems

ENTERTAINMENTS

Epitaph for a Tramp
Epitaph for a Dead Beat
Miss Doll, Go Home

Again—
For Sydney, for Duncan, for Toby

And for Trish Hoard

Painting is not done to decorate apartments.

PICASSO

If there wasn't death, I think you couldn't go on.

STEVIE SMITH

There are six floors in Novelist's apartment build- ing. Then again, the paved inner airshaft courtyard is at basement level, making seven.

And then the roof.

From high up on the Sistine ceiling scaffolding, Michelangelo was known to now and then drop things—brooms, even fairly long boards.

Most frequently, it appeared, when the pope hap- pened to be lurking below for a glimpse at his latest efforts.

When I die, I open a bordello. You know what is a bordello, no? But against every one of you—all—I lock shut the door.

Said Arturo Toscanini, to a recalcitrant orchestra.

As a talisman for the future while still young and penniless, Balzac once sketched a large blank representation of a picture frame on one of his garret walls—and designated it *Painting by Raphael.*

Old. Tired. Sick. Alone. Broke.

A Frenchman in Delft in 1663, looking to purchase inexpensive art, was shown a Vermeer—on display in a pastry shop.

Almost certainly being held there as security for a debt of Vermeer's to the baker.

Keats stayed up all night on the occasion when he actually did first look into Chapman's Homer—and then composed his sonnet so swiftly that he was able to messenger it to a friend to read before breakfast.

Van Gogh, in a letter from Arles, some few weeks after having presented a piece of his ear to a woman in a brothel:

I went yesterday to see the girl I had gone to when I went astray in my wits. They told me that in this country things like that are not out of the ordinary.

Shelley, in a letter from Venice, on Byron's local *innamorati:*

The most ignorant, the most disgusting, the most bigoted; countesses smell so strongly of garlic, that an ordinary Englishman cannot approach them. Well, L.B. is familiar with the lowest sort of these women, the people his *gondolieri* pick up in the streets.

The unimaginably cramped cell in which St. John of the Cross was once imprisoned for months, beaten repeatedly and virtually starved, but where he nonetheless managed to compose some of his finest verses.

In a building that no longer exists—but can still be seen in El Greco's *View of Toledo.*

At least once, Flaubert informs readers that Emma Bovary's eyes are brown.

And several other times that they are black.

Sigmund Freud ran his household in such a rigidly patriarchal manner that his wife was literally expected to have spread the toothpaste on his brush each morning.

Old. Tired. Sick. Alone. Broke.

All of which obviously means that this is the last book Novelist is going to write.

Anton Chekhov died in Germany. His coffin arrived in Moscow in a freight car—distinctly labeled *Oysters.*

During their first four years in the East Hampton farmhouse where they would live until Pollock's death eleven years later, Jackson Pollock and Lee Krasner could not afford to install plumbing for heat and hot water.

Clarence Darrow went out of his way to inform A.E. Housman that he had recited two pieces of Housman's verse in avoiding the death penalty for Leopold and Loeb, even presenting Housman with a copy of the courtroom summation—which showed he had misquoted both.

Claude Monet's admission, after standing beside the deathbed of someone he had loved—that in spite of his grief he had spent much of the time analyzing which pigments comprised the color of her eyelids.

That day being come, Caesar going into the Senate house and speaking merrily unto the soothsayer, told him, The Ides of March be come. So be they, softly answered the soothsayer, but they are not yet past.

Says North's Plutarch.

A woman's body is not a mass of flesh in a state of decomposition, on which the green and purplish spots denote a complete state of cadaveric putrefaction.

An early critic presumed to inform Renoir.

The devil damn thee black, thou cream-fac'd loon;

Where gott'st thou that goose look?

—Wrote Shakespeare in *Macbeth.*

Now friend, what means thy change of countenance?

—Substituted William Davenant, in a rewritten version that was played for almost a century.

His last book. All of which also then gives Novelist carte blanche to do anything here he damned well pleases.

Which is to say, writing in his own personal genre, as it were.

The first one-man artist's exhibition on record—put together by Gustave Courbet in Paris in 1855.

In a tent just outside the official group show that had rejected him.

Preoccupied with a poem-in-progress, Paul Valéry once paused to glance at a proof sheet in the window of a printing shop, and then without quite realizing it began to mentally revise the lines.

Until it embarrassingly dawned on him that he was rewriting Racine and not himself.

Vermeer died in 1675. At which time one of his largest debts was, in fact, to a Delft baker.

For bread to feed a family of thirteen.

In November 1919, after a solar eclipse had irrefutably verified Einstein's concept of relativity, British physicists convened a major press gathering to announce it. The *New York Times* assigned the story to a man named Henry Crouch—a golf reporter.

An eccentric, dreamy, half-educated recluse in an out-of-the-way New England village cannot with impunity set at defiance the laws of gravitation and grammar. Oblivion lurks in the immediate neighborhood.

Said Thomas Bailey Aldrich of Emily Dickinson.

The William Sakspere of Gloucestershire—who was hanged as a thief in 1248.

Along with a letter of homage, Berlioz sent copies of the score of *The Damnation of Faust* to Goethe.

Who never responded.

Venomously malignant. Noxious. Blasphemous. Grotesque. Disgusting. Repulsive. Entirely bestial. Indecent.

Being among the critical greetings for *Leaves of Grass.*

Not to omit ithyphallic audacity.

Plus garbage.

Profound stupidity. Maniacal raving. Pure nonsense.

Among some for the best of Shelley.

Which was also called abominable.

Infantile. Absurd. Driveling. Nauseating.

Reserved for Wordsworth.

For the rain it raineth every day.

Actually, Goethe had been gratified by Berlioz' letter. But then showed the *Faust* score to a now long-forgotten minor German composer—who informed him it was valueless.

After the 1953 Laurence Olivier film of *The Beggar's Opera,* Britain's Inland Revenue Service repeatedly sent inquiries regarding an address for John Gay—from whom they had not received income tax returns.

1732, Gay was buried at Westminster Abbey in.

I like Mr. Dickens' books much better than yours, Papa.

Said one of Thackeray's daughters.

At the height of his career, Richard Brinsley Sheridan had become the owner of the Drury Lane Theater. And subsequently astonished everyone concerned by calmly drinking in a nearby coffeehouse when it went up in flames:

Surely a man may be allowed to take a glass of wine by his own fireside?

What would you think this artist puts on canvas? Whatever fills his mind. And what can be in the mind of a man who spends his life in the company of prostitutes of the lowest order?

Inquired a review of François Boucher by Denis Diderot in 1765—when libel was evidently an absent concept.

An unmanly sort of man whose love life seems to have been largely confined to crying in laps and playing house.

Auden called Poe.

After having been driven to distraction by an organ grinder across the street from his Rome apartment, Pietro Mascagni finally politely demonstrated to the man how to operate the instrument less loudly.

Later to find him wearing a sign while performing: *Pupil of Mascagni.*

It takes a lot of time to be a genius, you have to sit around so much doing nothing, really doing nothing.

Said Gertrude Stein.

It is not amusing, it is not interesting, it is not good for one's mind.

Said T.S. Eliot—*re* Stein's prose.

Whistler, intending to show someone a new painting in his studio—who would always step in first and turn every other canvas to the wall.

Jackie Robinson had already played major league baseball for eight years before the Metropolitan Opera saw fit to ask Marian Anderson, then fifty-seven, to become its first black performer.

A full half-century after Marie Curie died from exposure to radiation, the very cookbooks she had once used were found to remain contaminated.

The courtesan Laïs, who once asserted that she knew nothing at all about the alleged wisdom of poets and philosophers—except that they knocked at her door as frequently as anyone else.

No philosopher has ever influenced the attitudes of even the street he lived on.

Said Voltaire.

Nonlinear. Discontinuous. Collage-like. An assemblage.

I do not see why exposition and description are a necessary part of a novel.

Said Ivy Compton-Burnett.

I am quite content to go down to posterity as a scissors and paste man.

Said Joyce.

Rilke was raised as a girl—in girl's clothing—until he started school at the age of seven.

The Rilke who would later devotedly collect lace.

And maintain apartments habitually overflowing with roses.

García Lorca's ten or eleven months in New York City—during which he apparently did not learn two dozen words of English.

I am not an orphan on the earth, so long as this man lives on it.

Said Gorky *re* Tolstoy.

What sort of *Christian* life is this, I should like to know? He hasn't a drop of love for his children, for me, or for anyone but himself.

Reads a contrasting view from Sofia Tolstoy's diary.

People speak of naturalism in opposition to modern painting. Where and when has anyone ever seen a natural work of art?

Asked Picasso.

How miraculous it was, noted Diogenes, that whenever one felt that sort of urge, one could readily masturbate.

But conversely how disheartening that one could not simply rub one's stomach when hungry.

The very possibly not apocryphal tale that David Hume, always grossly overweight, once went down on one knee to propose marriage—and could not get back up.

Dante walked with a stoop.

Said Boccaccio.

Coleridge fell off horses.

Albert Camus had already purchased a train ticket, between the Vaucluse and Paris, when he made a last-minute decision to accept a ride with Michel Gallimard—which would end in the crash that killed them both.

How many times before his own death twenty-eight years later would René Char recall that Camus and Gallimard had invited him to drive north with them also—but that he had decided their car would be too crowded?

An upstart crow, Robert Greene famously called Shakespeare in 1592.

A pair of crows, Pindar called Simonides and Bacchylides—two millennia earlier.

As Lucian wrote of Helen's face having launched a thousand ships—1,400 years before Marlowe.

I am he that aches with amorous love.

Wrote Whitman.
Walter, leave off.
Wrote D.H. Lawrence.
Elizabeth Barrett Browning's son Pen slept in her bedroom until her death. When he was twelve.
This man will never accomplish anything.
Said Pope Leo X—of Leonardo da Vinci.
This boy will come to nothing.
Said Freud's father.
The cave on Salamis where for a time, ca. 410BC, Euripides lived and wrote.
The ancient clay pot discovered there in 1997—inscribed with the first six letters of his name.
That scoundrel Brahms. What a giftless bastard!
Tchaikovsky's diary says.
Always give a moment's pause when happening to remember—that Shakespeare had three brothers.
One of whom was a haberdasher.
The justice Abe Fortas, once doing Pablo Cassals the favor of transporting his cello from San Juan to New York for repairs—
And purchasing two adjacent first-class seats for the flight.
Le Douanier Rousseau, contemplating Cézanne's work for the first time, at a memorial exhibition in 1907:
I could have finished those paintings for him.

Men who do not devote their lives to pursuing wisdom will be reborn as women.

Determined Plato.

People who marry young will have female children.

Determined Aristotle.

So difficult and opaque it is, I am not certain what it is I print.

Said John Donne's very publisher about the first edition of his verse.

Modigliani's repeated insistence that Rembrandt was a Jew.

The possibility that his own mother was a collateral descendant of Spinoza.

Shakespeare's sister Joan—the only sibling to survive him, and a relatively indigent widow.

Whose welfare he took care to safeguard in his will.

Oliver Goldsmith, who was well-liked by virtually everyone who knew him—and died owing money to all of them.

Was ever a poet so trusted before? asked Samuel Johnson.

As a schoolboy, Luther was once flogged fifteen times in one morning for being unprepared with a conjunction.

Bizet died only three months after the premiere of *Carmen*—convinced it was an irremediable failure.

Next to the originator of a great sentence is the first quoter of it.

Said Emerson.

Stories happen only to people who know how to tell them.

Said Thucydides.

Depressed at the apparent lack of interest in one of his early still lifes, Matisse visited his dealer to retrieve it, only to learn that it had been purchased after all.

By Picasso.

A novel of intellectual reference and allusion, so to speak minus much of the novel.

And thus in which Novelist will say more about himself only when he finds no way to evade doing so, but rarely otherwise.

A time came when none of us could use the figure without mutilating it.

Mark Rothko once said.

Rupert Brooke's obituary in the *London Times,* at his death in the Aegean in World War I, was written by Winston Churchill.

Dostoievsky's four years as a convict at hard labor in Siberia—where he lived always in a barracks.

Meaning that for four full years he essentially never had one moment to himself.

He is not writing about something; he is writing something.

Said Samuel Beckett, *re* Joyce.

He never thinks *about* something; he thinks something.

Said Hannah Arendt, *re* Heidegger.

Not bright colors. Good drawing.

Titian said.

The great early nineteenth-century diva Catalani, in retirement in Paris, is told she has an anonymous visitor. At the door, a young woman bows her head in modesty:

Madame, I have come to ask your blessing. My name is Jenny Lind.

Fragonard, ignored and forgotten in later life, but painting nonetheless:

I would paint with my backside if necessary.

Realizing that as recently as in the case of Haydn, musicians under the patronage of royalty were still treated as servants—and still wore livery.

An even earlier dismayed recognition of Dürer's, while visiting in Venice in 1506:

Here I am a gentleman—and at home a mere parasite.

We advise no woman to read this book.

Said a first review of *Père Goriot.*

Truly, young girls and women about to become mothers would do well, if they are wise, to run away from this spectacle.

Said another, of Manet's *Olympia.*

At twenty-two, William Faulkner was a special student for a semester at the University of Mississippi—and was given a grade of D in English.

Corresponding with him in later years, Allen Tate became aware that Faulkner habitually signed his letters with only his last name—and mentioned that English nobility signed letters that way.

Faulkner never wrote to Tate again.

The sun is as wide as a man's foot.

Judged Heraclitus.

The size of a foot soldier's shield.

Lucretius decided.

Einstein was reading Kant's *Critique of Pure Reason* at thirteen.

Kant died in 1804. More than seven hundred different authors had published books and/or essays on his work in the preceding two decades.

Clodia, whom Catullus immortalized as Lesbia in his verse—and Cicero dismissed as what can best be translated as that farthing whore.

Every half-quarter of an Hour, a glass of Sack must be sent of an errand into his Guts, to tell his Brains they must come up quickly, and help out with a line.

Said a minor poet named Robert Wilde of Ben Jonson at work.

He kept bottles of wine at his lodgeing, and many times he would drinke liberally by himselfe to refresh his spirits, and exalt his Muse.

Similarly said John Aubrey of Andrew Marvell.

Christina Rossetti's practice of pasting heavy paper over irreligious passages in Swinburne.

E.g., a line referring to the supreme evil, God, unquote, in *Atalanta in Calydon.*

January 23, 1931, Anna Pavlova died on.

Renoir, well into his forties and still impoverished.

So thin it wrung your heart, a woman friend remembered.

Yehudi Menuhin performed as a soloist with the San Francisco Orchestra at the age of seven.

A dogged attempt to cover the universe with mud.

E.M. Forster called *Ulysses.*

Conscious and calculated indecency.

Virginia Woolf settled for.

Along with *tosh*—presumably signifying something akin to twaddle.

So preoccupied was Thomas Hobbes with geometry that he sometimes diagrammed propositions on his bedsheets.

Or inked them on his thigh.

Unendurable to the music lover, Beethoven was becoming.

Said a contemporary critic—of the *Eroica.*

A depraved ear.

Said one of the same—of Mozart's D-minor quartet.

Item, I give unto my wife my second-best bed with the furniture.

So often unnoted—that by law Anne automatically also received one-third of the estate.

Hart Crane's leap into the Caribbean—

And the insistence of one of the witnesses that he was pulled under by sharks.

I was much impressed by the chalk-white face with the swollen purple lips, and felt confident he had been brooding over the Crucifixion all night, or some other holy torture.

Said William Empson *re* sightings of Eliot, ca. 1930.

Who will buy me, who will buy me,
rid me of my cares?

Very nearly three hundred times, in *Oliver Twist,* Fagin is referred to as *the Jew.*

Curiously leaving Dickens nonetheless distressed when the book was taken as anti-Semitic.

Hegel, asking Schelling's advice about a town to settle in, and listing his chief requirements:

A good library and *ein gutes Bier*—a good beer.

Women were not granted degrees at Oxford until as late as 1920.

A head of hair like an umbrella.

Someone said Berlioz had.

Like a great primeval forest.

Heinrich Heine made it.

Schopenhauer's mother Johanna wrote novels. When she playfully belittled his own first book, Schopenhauer told her it would still be available long after hers were forgotten.

Indeed, the entire first printing would still be, Johanna Schopenhauer said.

Rodin's monument to Victor Hugo—which was rejected by the group that commissioned it.

Rodin's monument to Balzac—which was rejected by the group that commissioned it.

Rodin's monument to Whistler—et cetera.

Quoth Charlie Parker, showing someone the veins at which he injected heroin:

This one's my Cadillac—

And this one's my house.

Adolf Hitler's occupation, as listed on his tax returns until such time as he officially became Germany's chancellor:

Writer.

Madame Butterfly is fifteen years old.

Rereading a Raymond Chandler novel in which Philip Marlowe stops in for a ten-cent cup of coffee.

Old enough to remember when the coffee would have cost half that.

Vosdanig Manoog Adoian, who changed his name to Arshile Gorky—and simultaneously announced that he was a nephew of the writer.

Not knowing that the other Gorky was not really named Gorky either.

Lying on his back in a field for hours, sometimes from almost before dawn or until latest evening, memorizing the light in the sky.

Reads a friend's recollection of Claude Lorrain.

The sky can never be merely a background.

Said Alfred Sisley.

Imperialist bourgeois and decadent counterrevolutionary tendencies.

Both Shostakovich and Prokofiev were accused of at one time or another by Soviet authorities.

God gave me the money.

Unquote. John D. Rockefeller.

The noblest title in the world is that of having been born a Frenchman, said Napoleon.

Born in Corsica—of Italian ancestry.

Alexei Maximovitch Peshkov.

Stronger than a man, simpler than a child, her nature stood alone. I have seen nothing like it, but indeed, I have never seen her parallel in anything.

Said Charlotte Brontë of Emily.

Vespasian, who is remembered for having built the Colosseum.

But who also established Rome's first public urinals.

The interrelationship of Picasso and Braque during Cubism:

Like being roped together on a mountain, Braque said.

Stalin read Hemingway.

His ferocious egoism revolts me every time I think of it.

Said the wife Gauguin left behind.

Cézanne's *Old Woman of the Beads*—

Posed for by a servant he took in basically out of charity, and who then stole and shredded much of his underwear—which he allowed her to sell back to him as rags for his brushes.

Almost forgetting Emily Brontë's mastiff—which slept at the door of her room for years, after her death.

That harmonious plagiary and miserable flatterer, whose cursed hexameters were drilled into me at Harrow.

Byron spoke of Virgil as.

Benny Goodman once cancelled an engagement at the Hotel New Yorker on the very day it was scheduled to start—when he was informed that all black musicians connected with his band would have to come and go through the hotel kitchen.

It seems a great pity that they allowed her to die a natural death.

Said Mark Twain—of Jane Austen.

I've been shitting, so 'tis said, nigh twenty-two years through the same old hole, which is not yet frayed one bit.

Wrote Mozart to his cousin Anna Maria Thekla.

With whom he may or may not have had an affair.

Émile Zola's terror of thunder and lightning—so extreme that he not only shut all windows and lit every nearby lamp, but even sometimes blindfolded himself.

Human inventions, set up to terrify and enslave mankind.

Tom Paine called religions.

Senseless and criminal bigotry.

Nehru saw in them.

I thought I had done that already.

Said Mallarmé—at the first talk of Debussy setting *L'Après-midi d'un Faune* to music.

Einstein's honorary degree from Harvard.

Evidently at the recommendation of an alumnus named Franklin D. Roosevelt.

I wish you good night, but first shit into your bed.

Reads another Mozart letter to Anna Maria.

Leering effrontery, *Harper's Weekly* once accused Matisse of.

He'll probably never write a good play again.

Responded George Bernard Shaw—on being told that Eugene O'Neill had given up drinking.

Willem de Kooning was twenty-two when he emigrated to the United States from Rotterdam—as a stowaway on a British freighter.

The oddity that Velazquez and Picasso, surely two of the three greatest Spanish-born painters, each used his mother's name rather than his father's.

Among the fragments of ancient Greek literature unearthed in Egypt, where the climate and the soil preserve them extraordinarily, there is almost twice as much material about Homer as anyone else.

And five times as much Plato as Aristotle.

Andrew Lang's indignation over a mild blasphemy in *Tess of the d'Urbervilles.*

A gentleman who turned Christian for half an hour, Hardy dismissed him as.

Spinoza, who spent his last years in a single attic room in The Hague—and slept in some variant or other of what is now called a Murphy bed.

Spinoza. Shoving or yanking or hoisting or whatever, to force the unstable whatchamacallit up against the wall each morning.

Unworthy of the poets' corner of a country newspaper.

Yeats called Wilfred Owen.

No one expressed interest in publishing Shelley's *Defense of Poetry* until almost twenty years after his death.

No one expressed interest in publishing *Billy Budd* until thirty-three years after Melville's.

Every Grass, Emily Dickinson once refers to.

While also contriving:

The Grass so little has to do
I wish I were a Hay—

Balzac had written eighty-five novels in his *Comédie humaine*—with *fifty* more already planned—before dying at the age of fifty-one.

Adam was bored alone; then Adam and Eve were bored together.

Said Kierkegaard.

Amid the clutter of multilingual graffiti beside the door to the St. Petersburg garret that is alleged to be the one Dostoievsky used as a model for Raskolnikov's:

Don't do it, Rodya!

Old enough to remember when they were still called penny postcards.

And a letter cost three cents.

Like the daily *New York Times.*

Trying to calculate the odds against two poets as talented as Sylvia Plath and Anne Sexton taking part in the same university writing workshop at the same time—and with an instructor of the stature of Robert Lowell.

And/or the chances that within a decade and a half both would be suicides.

The next best thing to God.

Edna O'Brien called literature.

Manet made two separate copies of Delacroix's *Dante and Virgil in Hell.*

Cézanne made six.

July 6, 1971, Louis Armstrong died on.

In Elizabethan London—the heads of executed criminals on spikes on London Bridge.

Wondering how frequently Shakespeare or Marlowe or Jonson might have paused to watch their eyeballs being plucked out by kites or crows.

Bertrand Russell wrote his *Introduction to Mathematical Philosophy* while serving six months in Brixton prison for pacifist protests during World War I.

Enrico Fermi once wrote an entire full-length textbook on atomic physics in pencil—without an eraser.

Eighty-eight years after his death, almost fifty Turner canvases, rolled up and inexplicably mislabeled as tarpaulins, were come upon by sheerest chance in National Gallery storage rooms.

Valladolid, Christopher Columbus died in.

After drinking heavily, Philip of Macedon once pronounced a judgment that an elderly woman said she would appeal.

Appeal to whom, when I am your king?

To my king when he is sober.

Philip reversed his judgment.

Ambition for wealth is the enemy of artistic excellence.

Warned Leon Battista Alberti—in 1436.

O painter, take care lest the greed for gain prove a stronger incentive than the desire for renown, for this latter achievement is a far greater thing than riches.

Wrote Leonardo two generations afterward.

George Moore once walked in on Swinburne, uninvited, to find him striding back and forth declaiming Aeschylus at the top of his voice—stark naked.

The first opera Toscanini ever saw, at the age of four, was *Un Ballo in Maschera.*

The last opera Toscanini ever conducted, at the age of eighty-seven, was *Un Ballo in Maschera.*

A sixth-century AD sporting event, as Novelist remembers it from *Beowulf:*

Holding one's opponent under water until he is drowned.

24

Fenimore Cooper used almost eleven hundred Shakespeare quotations as epigraphs and/or chapter headings in his thirty-plus novels.

My music is best understood by children and animals.

Said Stravinsky.

The thought of Rembrandt's bankruptcy, at fifty. Of his possessions—his *paintings*—being sold for whatever pittance they might bring. Of Rembrandt himself being evicted from his home.

Rembrandt.

Now Dawn arose from her couch beside the lordly Tithonos, to bear light to the immortals and to mortal men.

Says the opening of Book XI of the *Iliad.*

Now Dawn arose from her couch beside the lordly Tithonos, to bear light to the immortals and to mortal men.

Says the opening of Book V of the *Odyssey.*

He had the finest ear, perhaps, of any English poet; he was also undoubtedly the stupidest.

Said Auden of Tennyson.

Not conspicuously intelligent.

Auden added *re* Yeats.

Advice from Arthur Schnabel to the younger Vladimir Horowitz:

When a piece gets difficult, make faces.

The greatest love specialist in the world, Samuel Goldwyn called Freud.

While offering him $100,000 to supervise or even write a romantic story for Hollywood.

Freud at the time was asking fees of twenty dollars an hour. He dismissed Goldwyn with a one-sentence note.

Discovering that the Cynara to whom Ernest Dowson had been faithful in his fashion was in fact a London waitress.

Wagner has some fine moments. But some bad quarters of an hour.

Said Rossini.

The color of cognac.

Rodin described Suzanne Valadon's hair as.

The imagination will not perform until it has been flooded by a vast torrent of reading.

Announced Petronius.

You have to read fifteen hundred books in order to write one.

Flaubert put it.

Fra Filippo Lippi was past fifty, and the chaplain of a convent, when he abducted the nun by whom he would have two children—one of the same being the Filippino who would follow him as an artist.

Albert Pinkham Ryder dressed so shabbily that now and again people attempted to hand him loose change as he walked the streets near Greenwich Village.

The artist must live to paint and not paint to live. He should not sacrifice his ideals to a landlord.

Ryder said.

Nobody wants his mule and wagon stalled on the same track the Dixie Limited is roaring down.

Said Flannery O'Connor—apropos of being a Southern writer as a contemporary of Faulkner's.

Among the many paintings in her Paris flat, Gertrude Stein had two exceptional Picassos.

If there were a fire, and I could save only one picture, it would be those two. Unquote.

August 15, 1967, René Magritte died on.

Victor Hugo constantly made notes about everything—and would turn aside in the middle of a conversation to scribble down something he himself had just said that he realized he might possibly later be able to use.

O Lord, who art hidden in the clouds and behind the cobbler's house—

Commenced a prayer voiced by Marc Chagall as a boy in Vitebsk.

The nature of genius is to provide idiots with ideas twenty years later.

Said Louis Aragon.

Novelist's isolation—ever increasing as the years pass also.

Days on which he is aware of speaking to no one at all, for example, except perhaps a checkout clerk, or his letter carrier, or some basically anonymous fellow tenant in the elevator.

Matt Arnold, he was commonly called.

Jack Galsworthy.

The grete poete of Ytaille.

Chaucer referred to Dante as—in the late four-teenth century.

Though there would be no English translation of the *Divine Comedy* until 1785.

Shakespeare's name, you may depend on it, stands absurdly too high and will go down.

Insisted Byron.

Was he Christian, Jewish, or atheist? Samuel Beckett was once asked in a Dublin courtroom. To which:

None of the three.

The extant application for a reader's ticket at the British Museum signed by Arthur Rimbaud on March 25, 1873, attesting that he has read the regulations for the Reading Room and that he is not under twenty-one years of age—when in truth he was still only eighteen.

Catullus, informing friends that he is broke:

With nothing but cobwebs in my wallet.

The Shakespeare of the lunatic asylum.

An early French critic called Dostoievsky.

Foul. Like a rat, slithering along in hate. He is not nice.

Being D.H. Lawrence's later view.

The concept of life after death should be empathically promulgated by the state, Plato said.

If only so that soldiers would be willing to die in battle.

George Washington left no children of his own.

A great-granddaughter of Martha's, by way of her earlier marriage, married Robert E. Lee.

The most repulsive thing I ever saw or heard in my life.

Said Clara Schumann of *Tristan und Isolde.*

Plutarch, who relinquished fame and power in Rome to live quietly and do his writing in Chaeronea, near Delphi.

A small town that would have been even smaller if I left.

Brave translunary things.

Michael Drayton saw in Marlowe.

Intemperate & of a cruel hart.

Thomas Kyd noted of him instead.

For half a dozen years, in his middle and late fifties, Oskar Kokoschka was forced to turn out little other than watercolors—because he generally could not spare the few dollars for oils and canvas.

Cry, art, cry, and loudly lament.

No one, any longer, desires you.

Woe is me.

—Lettered Lucas Moser, a minor German painter, onto an altarpiece in 1431.

Fortune favors the brave, says Virgil.

Presumably aware that Terence had said it earlier.

Brunelleschi once carved a wood crucifix by which Donatello was so impressed that he could only gape in astonishment—while also spilling the apron full of eggs he had been bringing to Brunelleschi's studio for their lunch.

Tennyson was once so drunk at the end of a London dinner that he started to leave by way of the fireplace.

I sing, as the Boy does by the Burying Ground—because I am afraid.

El Greco. Vermeer. Dieric Bouts. Frans Hals.

Each of whom was essentially forgotten for at least two centuries.

Or longer.

Bombastic nonsense. Concepts bordering on madness. Humbug.

Schopenhauer found in Hegel.

The anecdote, passed on as genuine, about Beaumont and Fletcher once being angrily accused of high treason by strangers in a tavern who had become convinced they were plotting to kill the king—when in actuality they had been discussing the outline of a new play.

He had often regretted opening his mouth, said Simonides.

But he could not recall having ever caused any major catastrophe by keeping it shut.

Literature is the art of writing something that will be read twice.

Said Cyril Connolly.

England expects that every man will do his duty.

Every *man,* on Nelson's flagship the *Victory,* incidentally including boys of ten and twelve, some having been caught up by press gangs.

During most of his adult life, Joshua Reynolds made use of an ear trumpet.

And in his final years became almost totally blind.

Beethoven's unkempt, laundry-strewn Vienna flat.

While beneath the piano, recollected at least one visitor, his chamber pot—unemptied.

John Locke died while sitting in a drawing room listening to someone read from the Psalms.

Novalis died while listening to a relative play the piano.

The wintry conscience of a generation.

V.S. Pritchett called George Orwell.

A poem by Theocritus written in Alexandria ca. 270BC—

Complaining that the streets were too crowded.

Antonin Artaud spent nine of his last eleven years in insane asylums.

For decades, next door to the building in The Hague that had housed Spinoza's attic:

The Spinoza Saloon.

Man is the only animal that knows he must die.

Said Voltaire.

St.-John Perse. Who was translated into English by Eliot.

And into German by Rilke.

September 9, 1960, Jussi Bjoerling died on.

Looked into by church authorities at Arnstadt in 1706, where Bach at twenty was organist:

By what right he had recently caused the strange maiden to be invited into the organ loft?

One day I wrote her name upon the strand.

A Man of Genius whose heart is perverted.

Wordsworth called Byron.

The most vulgar-minded genius that ever produced a great effect in literature.

George Eliot phrased it.

After devoting years to the score for *Pelléas et Méllisande,* Debussy played it through for Maurice Maeterlinck, on whose play it was based. Maeterlinck repeatedly dozed off in his chair.

Henry Moore was gassed in the trenches in World War I.

The *Bateau-Lavoir,* the legendary former Montmartre piano factory broken up into artists' studios, where Picasso contrived any number of his early masterpieces—while living with no running water and only one communal toilet.

And which sixty years later was named a national historical monument—only to burn to the ground a few months afterward.

Continental degeneracy, Thomas Jefferson was several times condemned for.

Because of a chef who had been trained in Paris, Patrick Henry explained.

The bleak image Novelist is granted of himself as he asks a question of a local pharmacist—and becomes aware of the woman contemplating the conspicuously threadbare and even ragged ends of his coat sleeves.

Writing is the only profession where no one considers you ridiculous if you earn no money.

Said Jules Renard.

Gilda, in *Rigoletto.* Whom Mattiwilda Dobbs sang as at the Metropolitan two years after Marian Anderson had done Ulrica in *Un Ballo in Maschera* —making her the first black soprano to perform there in a romantic role opposite a white tenor.

Jack Dempsey's claim that he was partly Jewish.

Via a great-great-grandmother named Rachael Solomon.

Chaucer's personal library. The guess being forty volumes, presumably most of them in Latin.

Leonardo's. Known to have contained thirty-seven.

Joseph Conrad spoke English with such a thick, partially French accent that people often had extraordinary difficulty in understanding him.

Le Bateau ivre.

Margot Fonteyn, in an early discussion of women's liberation:

Will it mean I have to lift Nureyev, instead of vice versa?

Xerxes: Go, and tell those madmen to deliver up their arms.

Leonidas: Go, and tell Xerxes to come and take them.

George Sand, *re* an 1873 literary evening:

Flaubert talks with animation and humor, but all to do with himself. Turgenev, who is much more interesting, can hardly get a word in.

Parodying without taste or skill. Very near the limits of coherence.

Said the *Times Literary Supplement* of *The Waste Land.*

Unintelligible, the borrowings cheap and the notes useless.

Said the *New Statesman and Nation.*

So much waste paper.

Summed up the *Manchester Guardian.*

Kant's irrationally compulsive 3:30PM walk, which it is said he forswore only once in thirty years—on the day when the post brought him a first copy of Rousseau's *Émile.*

A German singer! I would as soon hear my horse neigh.

Said Frederick the Great, insisting upon Italian performers for opera in Berlin.

A.E. Housman. Who spent most of his adult life as a professor of Latin.

After originally failing his final exams at Oxford.

What, still alive at twenty-two,
A fine upstanding lad like you?

From the beginnings of the legend of Michelangelo's sense of his own worth:

He treats the Pope as the King of France himself would not dare to treat him—unquote.

John Donne, near death, as recorded by Izaak Walton:

His sickness had left him but so much flesh as did only cover his bones.

Pausing to speculate about the plumbing of the era—and wondering how frequently Shakespeare might have bathed.

Or even two centuries later, Jane Austen.

Józef Teodor Konrad Nalecz Korzeniowski.

Rat-eyed, Virginia Woolf called Somerset Maugham.

An old parrot, Christopher Isherwood saw instead.

February 6, 1916, Rubén Darío died on.

Everyone honors the wise. The citizens of Mytilene honored Sappho even though she was a woman.

Said Aristotle.

He who has money is wise. And handsome. And can sing well also.

Says a Yiddish proverb.

Walt Whitman's claim—never in any way verified—that he had fathered at least six illegitimate children.

The woman named Mercy Rogers, who in the early 1920s when the subject was relatively new, read practically every available book on psychoanalysis—and then put her head into the oven.

Certain men have such command of their bowels, that they can break wind continuously, at their pleasure, so as to produce the effect of singing.

Insisted Saint Augustine.

Englishwomen have big feet.

Nietzsche determined.

Man: But a little soul bearing about a corpse.

Marcus Aurelius says Epictetus said.

Richie Wagner, Charles Ives amused himself by calling him.

Truman Streckfus Persons, Truman Capote's birth-certificate name was.

He wore a grey suit, black shoes, white shirt, tie and vest. His appearance never changed. He came down in the morning in this suit, and he would still be wearing it the last thing at night.

Said John Huston, *re* Sartre.

Einstein often went without socks.

The final blowup of what was once a remarkable, if minor, talent.

Clifton Fadiman said of *Absalom, Absalom!*

Curiously dull, furiously commonplace, and often meaningless.

Alfred Kazin said of Faulkner in general.

Me, tell you? I don't know anything about it. I laid down face up and began to sing. Children came like water.

British troops reached Belsen, the first Nazi concentration camp to be reported on, in April of 1945.

Forty thousand starving and/or dying prisoners. Ten thousand unburied corpses, corded like wood.

It is my duty to describe something beyond the imagination of mankind, began the dispatch to the *London Times.*

I pray you to believe what I have said about Buchenwald.

Pleaded Edward R. Murrow, on trans-Atlantic radio, after reporting much the same soon thereafter.

Our worst century so far.

Elizabeth Bishop called that one.

Everything is supposed to be very quiet after a massacre, and it always is, except for the birds.

Says a line in *Slaughterhouse-Five.*

Huckleberry Finn was once banned from the children's room of the Brooklyn Public Library because—Novelist is quoting here—Huck said sweat when he should have said perspiration.

Wondering if the myth of Dedalus and Icarus has ever been thought of as the first science fiction story?

The only thing that could sound worse in an orchestra than a flute—would be two flutes.

Said Cherubini.

Jean Genet was arrested for the first time—for theft—at the age of ten.

David Garrick's explanation for the excessive number of bawdy plays on the late eighteenth-century English stage:

Because the first great ruling passion of actors is to eat.

E.M. Forster's astonishment at learning that telephone wires were not hollow.

Old enough to remember when any number of people seemed to believe something similar—or at the least felt it necessary to shout, when confronted with long distance.

Five or six lunatics, the contributors to the first Impressionist exhibition were called by *Le Figaro.*

Heine read Plutarch's *Lives* for the first time when quite young.

And said it made him wish to leap onto a stallion and ride off to conquer France.

William Blake's emphatically avowed lack of interest in sex.

The Red and the Black, John F. Kennedy's favorite novel was.

According to Vasari, Leonardo devoted four full years to painting the *Mona Lisa.*

The *Mona Lisa* covers a slight fraction more than five and one-half square feet of surface.

Sarah Bernhardt lost a leg at seventy-one.

And one year later was performing for French troops at the front in World War I.

On a wall in Freud's waiting room in Vienna:
Bernhardt's photo.

A man either utterly devoid of sense or one who takes his listeners for fools.

An early critic called Schoenberg.

A debris of sour jokes, stage anger, dirty words, synthetic loneliness, and the sort of antic behavior children fall into when they know they are losing our attention.

The *New Yorker* called *Catch-22.*

Lo, there is just appeared a truly classic work.

Wrote Horace Walpole—within one day of the publication of Gibbon's *Decline and Fall.*

Rhoda Broughton's *Dear Faustina,* from 1897. Is it the first lesbian novel in English?

Jean Cocteau's addiction to opium.

Francis Thompson's.

Modigliani's. To opium, hashish, and drink.

People who more immediately think of Meursault as a character in Camus rather than as a dry white Burgundy.

Czar Alexis, father of Peter the Great, who in the mid – seventeenth century ordered the destruction of all musical instruments in Russia.

Pope Leo XII. Who in the 1820s issued an edict forbidding the waltz in Rome.

Magnificently, awe-inspiringly ugly.

Henry James called George Eliot.

Aujourd'hui, maman est morte. Ou peut-etre hier, je ne sais pas.

Not until a year after his burial at Sag Harbor did someone notice that the title of *The Recognitions* was misspelled on the back of William Gaddis's headstone.

The true/untrue/pleasant-in-either-case tale that Salvador Dalí had been noticed gazing in almost hypnotic fascination at a melting wedge of

Camembert on a dinner table not long before painting the limp watches in *The Persistence of Memory.*

I am extremely happy—until further notice.

Says a letter of Berlioz about his romance with Harriet Smithson.

An alcoholic is someone you don't like who drinks almost as much as you do.

Said Dylan Thomas.

But I'm not so think as you drunk I am.

Suggested J.C. Squire.

The seeming likelihood that Pythagoras is implying that the world is round—in the mid – sixth century BC.

He had not escaped the common penalties of transgressing the laws of strict purity, wrote Alexander Thayer *re* Beethoven.

Which is to say—he had syphilis.

Guillaume Apollinaire authored a considerable amount of art criticism, particularly as an early champion of Cubism.

While at the same time being incapable of distinguishing a Rubens from a Rembrandt, Braque commented.

Thales of Miletus, when his mother begged him to marry: It is too soon.

After she permitted him some delay: It is too late.

Once, watching a ceremonial procession near the Vatican, Samuel Morse failed to remove his hat—and had it roughly knocked off by a papal guard.

And became vociferously anti-Catholic thereafter.

June 7, 1843, Friedrich Hölderlin died on.

Be informed, Christian, that after the devil thou hast no enemy more cruel, more venomous, more violent, than the Jew.

Pronounced Luther.

World War II—started by sixty kikes.

Pronounced Ezra Pound.

Kill the Jews wherever you find them. This pleases God.

Pronounced the Grand Mufti of Jerusalem—well before a State of Israel existed.

While also citing Adolf Eichmann as both gallant and noble.

To sit for John Singer Sargent, Yeats appeared in a velvet coat and a billowing bow tie—and then carefully arranged a lock of hair to fall across his forehead.

All this to remind himself of his importance as an artist, Sargent said he said.

The last time anyone mentioned William Saroyan.

Eleusis, Aeschylus was born in.

Colonus, Sophocles.

Salamis, Euripides.

T.S. Eliot missed military service in World War I because of a hernia.

Pound had astigmatism.

Andrea del Castagno's masterwork, a last supper, was painted at the Convent of Sant'Apollonia in Florence in 1447.

And was not seen by other artists for four hundred years—because of the convent being closed to laypersons.

The state should keep me, Schubert once suggested. I have come into the world for no purpose but to compose.

Now that a certain portion of mankind does not believe at all in the existence of the gods, a rational legislation ought to do away with the oaths.

Wrote Plato—2,310 years before an act of the United States Congress added the phrase *under God* to the Pledge of Allegiance.

Suddenly taking a moment to wonder—does anyone any longer make use of Morse code?

I pay well. But the wenches are all whores and pigs.

Says a Michelangelo letter about a servant problem.

André Malraux had reached Spain within two days of the start of the Civil War in 1936.

Living the classic impoverished artist's life while a student in Milan, Giacomo Puccini was once forced to pawn his overcoat—as he allows one of his characters to do in *La Bohème.*

In *El Diario de Madrid,* February 1799, a first advertisement for prints of Goya's *Caprichos:*

On sale at No. 1 Calle del Desengaño, the perfume and liquor store.

Beatrix Potter had to pay to publish *The Tale of Peter Rabbit.*

I am hungry. I am cold. When I grow up I want to be a German, and then I shall no longer be hungry and cold.

Wrote a Jewish youngster in the Warsaw Ghetto.

Not long before his death, Toulouse-Lautrec spent several months in a mental institution, being released only in care of a guardian whose portrait he then painted.

My keeper when I was mad, he inscribed it.

Ludwig Wittgenstein's shockingly limited aesthetic sensibilities in every area except music. His virtual *consecration* of third-rate American pulp fiction detective stories, for instance.

Or his unashamed admission that Carmen Miranda and Betty Hutton ranked as his two favorite film actresses.

The earliest known reference to London by name, dated as long ago as 6AD—in Tacitus.

Columbus, Mississippi, Tennessee Williams was born in.

In an Episcopal rectory.

Moments in which Novelist does something like leaving his desk to retrieve a book from across the room—and finding himself staring vacantly into the refrigerator.

Or tossing his keys into a drawer—without having opened the drawer.

In Meleager's first-century BC anthology of Greek verse, an epigram in honor of an extraordinary woman—

The one who slept with only one man in her life.

Gerard Manley Hopkins, on realizing that he feels a certain kinship with Whitman:

As he is a very great scoundrel this is not a very pleasant confession.

Don't go into Mr. McGregor's garden: your father had an accident there.

John von Neumann was twenty-nine when he was appointed to the Institute for Advanced Study at Princeton—for life.

André Gide had a sexless marriage with a first cousin.

In spite of his admitted homosexuality, he also had an illegitimate child by another woman.

In Vermeer's paintings, repeatedly, letters being read or written.

In the real world—not one known word of any sort in Vermeer's own hand.

Manet's earliest major canvas, *The Absinthe Drinker.*

The only absinthe drinker here is the painter who perpetrated this madness, said Couture.

I'd rather not sing than sing quiet.

Janis Joplin said.

The Hiroshima survivor who remembered rushing into the street amid the chaos and tripping over someone's severed head.

And hysterically calling out Excuse me.

A stark naked man standing in the rain with his eyeball in his hand.

Another survivor recalled.

The ashes of Shelley's heart. Which Trelawney had scooped from the flames when the corpse was burned on the beach at Viareggio in 1822, and which were passed on to Mary—and were found in her copy of *Adonais* after her death in 1851.

Any *asino* can conduct. But to make music, eh? Is *difficile!*

Said Toscanini.

Rubens, in his early sixties—with arthritis so severe that both hands were paralyzed.

Rubens.

I've never read Shakespeare because the print's too small.

Says someone in Odets.

Wondering how things worked at the Institute for Advanced Study. Come noon, might von Neumann casually poke his head into Einstein's office and ask if he felt like lunch?

J.D. Salinger was awarded five battle stars as a staff sergeant in the European Theater in World War II.

Evelyn Waugh saw combat as a major with British commando units in North Africa, Crete, and Yugoslavia.

The Medieval poet Probus, whom Walafrid Strabo deemed superior to Virgil or Horace or Ovid—and whom no one any longer knows anything whatsoever about.

Paganini's legendary showmanship. Which included sometimes deliberately breaking a string midway through a performance—and going on with only the remaining three.

Wallpaper, George Steiner dismissed much of Jackson Pollock as.

Extremely expensive wallpaper, Kenneth Rexroth made it.

Someone once asked Caruso if he considered himself the world's greatest tenor.

Not unless John McCormack has suddenly become a baritone, Caruso said.

Why Diogenes had been noticed begging alms from a statue, a citizen wished to know.

To get into practice at being ignored, Diogenes explained.

The so-called Wicked Bible. Dated London 1632.

In which the word *not* was omitted in the seventh commandment.

Samuel Johnson's compulsive inability to stroll past a picket fence without superstitiously touching each separate picket as he went.

Remembering that in the *Odyssey* Odysseus himself is not first seen until Book V.

And then is seen weeping.

Rudolph Valentino was dead at thirty-one.

Mithridates, he died old.

If you think you understand it, that only shows you don't know the first thing about it.

Said Niels Bohr *re* quantum mechanics.

In an era when singers frequently embellished music to their own taste, Rossini once complimented Adelina Patti on an aria from *The Barber of Seville*—and then asked her who the composer was.

Claude Lorrain's *Coast View with Acis and Galatea,* which Dostoievsky once saw in Dresden and writes in *A Raw Youth* of having dreamed about.

And writes in *The Possessed* of having dreamed about.

And writes in *The Dream of a Ridiculous Man* of having dreamed about.

Emily Dickinson's refusal to sit for a photographer.

Henrik Ibsen was virtually never known to take off his hat without immediately combing his hair—having even glued a small mirror inside the hat to make use of when he did so.

September 23, 1835, Vincenzo Bellini died on.

April 8, 1848, Gaetano Donizetti died on.

There was no memorial of any sort for Byron in Westminster Abbey until 1969.

Still always slightly surprised to recall—that John McCormack died an American citizen.

The so-called anarchist artist who in 1988 smeared a large X in his own blood on a wall in the Museum of Modern Art—and in the process splattered an adjacent Picasso.

I can't understand these chaps who go round American universities explaining how they write poems; it's like going round explaining how you sleep with your wife.

Quoth Philip Larkin.

The sound of Bix Beiderbecke's cornet:

Like a girl saying yes, Eddie Condon said.

The sound of Paul Desmond's alto saxophone:

Like a dry martini, being what Desmond himself said he wanted.

Exactly the right tone of thought and feeling to appeal to grocers.

Leslie Stephen credited Dickens with.

Napoleon was five feet six inches tall.

A dozen or fifteen years before much of the nudity in Michelangelo's *Last Judgment* would be concealed by papal order, a ranking Vatican cardinal voiced the first complaint about same.

And shortly discovered his own portrait on the wall—in hell.

As almost happened similarly to a prior in Milan after his complaints about Leonardo's apparent desultoriness in work on *The Last Supper* —complaints that abruptly ceased at Leonardo's hint regarding who might become the model for Judas.

Kindly see me safe up. As for coming down I shall shift for myself.

Said Sir Thomas More—being led to the gallows.

In Robert Schumann's diary, after a first meeting with Berlioz:

There is something very pleasant about his laugh.

Thou shalt commit adultery.

The brains of a ram, Shaw attributed to Sophocles.

Of a third-rate village policeman—to Brahms.

Poor England, when such a despicable abortion is named genius.

Said Thomas Carlyle of Charles Lamb.

Anybody can be nobody.

Said Eugene V. Debs.

Novelist's personal genre. For all its seeming fragmentation, nonetheless obstinately cross-referential and of cryptic interconnective syntax.

Wondering why one is surprised to realize that Thoreau was dead at forty-five.

A lament of Schopenhauer's:

Over how frequently the mere purchase of a book is mistaken for the appropriation of its contents.

Two pages of *The Mill on the Floss* are enough to start me crying.

Said Proust.

Sour of speech, averse to laughter, unable to be merry even over the wine, but what he writes is full of honey and the Sirens.

Says a line of uncertain attribution *re* Euripides.

Lope de Vega had at least three illegitimate children.

Gustav Klimt may have had as many as fourteen.

Though the courts recognized only four, in regard to his estate.

Utterly crazy about women.

Suidas says of Menander.

Looking at them in society, one fancies there's something in them, but there's nothing, nothing, nothing. No, don't marry, my dear fellow, don't marry.

Repulsive, an early *New York Times* review called Degas.

Pigs at the pastry cart.

John Updike called critics.

Says a 1796 London jestbook:

Shakespear seeing Ben Jonson in a necessary-house, with a book in his hand reading it very attentively, said he was sorry his memory was so bad, that he could not *sh-te* without a Book.

Dürer's *hausfrau* wife.

Whom he on occasion remanded to eat with their maid.

Lenin played tennis.

The sign in the window says *Pants Pressed Here.* But when you bring in your pants, you discover that it is the sign that is for sale.

Being Kierkegaard—on the typical obscurity of what normally passes for philosophy.

The first use of the phrase *stream of consciousness.*

In a review by May Sinclair of Dorothy Richardson's *Pointed Roofs*—in April 1918.

The remedies of all our diseases will be discovered after we are dead.

Assumed John Stuart Mill.

Charlotte has been writing a book, and it is much better than likely.

Announced the Reverend Patrick Brontë, in the mid-1840s, to his other offspring.

Karl Marx was for some years a London correspondent for Horace Greeley's *New York Tribune.*

Attempting to detour the young Thomas Aquinas from a career in the church, his family once arranged for a seductive woman to be sent to his rooms.

Whom he chased off with a flaming brand from his hearth.

　　Maid of Athens, ere we part,
　　Give, oh give me back my heart!

For a time, Rilke and Cocteau had apartments in the same Paris building—evidently without ever becoming acquainted.

Every passenger in the non-smoking section of a plane that crashed off Norway in 1948 was killed.

Bertrand Russell had been smoking—and was one of those able to swim to safety.

Ravel once composed music for Diaghilev that Diaghilev never used.

And which almost led to a duel between them.

April 23, 1554, Gaspara Stampa died on.

I don't very much enjoy looking at paintings in general. I know too much about them.

Said Georgia O'Keeffe.

Harvard was founded in 1636.

The University of Mexico—in 1553.

One of the most illiterate books of any merit ever published.

Edmund Wilson called *This Side of Paradise.*

Not a lovable man.

John O'Hara said of Scott Fitzgerald himself.

Occasions on which one has seen it transliterated as *Theodor* Dostoievsky.

A tea-time bore.

Dylan Thomas called Wordsworth.

A son of Einstein's died in a mental institution at fifty-five—having been confined there for a third of a century.

The relatively recent revelation that Einstein had also had an illegitimate daughter.

Unhesitatingly specifying Pound's anti-Semitism as the reason, Yevgeny Yevtushenko once refused to appear on the same podium with him at a literary event.

Teddy Dostoievsky?

The Duccio *Madonna and Child* purchased by the Metropolitan Museum in 2004 for more than $45,000,000.

Which is eight inches wide and eleven inches high.

Jan Peerce. Leonard Warren. Richard Tucker. Robert Merrill.

The Lower East Side. The Bronx. Williamsburg. Williamsburg.

Jacques Derrida failed his entrance exams to the École Normal Supérieure. Twice.

People are exasperated by poetry which they do not understand, and contemptuous of poetry which they understand without effort.

Said Eliot.

We cease to wonder at what we understand.

Said Johnson.

Sir Thomas Beecham once told an orchestra that a certain passage in Mozart should sound inno-cent—quote—like a breath of spring. It should float on the air like a voice from another world.

When the musicians stared emptily:

Oh, well, anyway, play it legato.

A real good guy.

William Carlos Williams called Emily Dickinson.

A bitchy little spinster.

Denise Levertov saw her as instead.

Géricault's intensity when at work on *The Raft of the Medusa:*

The mere sound of a smile could prevent him from painting, someone said.

Ingres' judgment that the finished version ought to have been removed from the Louvre or even hidden away altogether:

Is it in such horrors that we should find pleasure? Art should teach us nothing but the Beautiful!

If English was good enough for Jesus Christ, it's good enough for us.

Said a 1920s Texas governor opposed to the teaching of foreign languages.

Persia, as it was still then called, Doris Lessing was born in.

Nobody comes. Nobody calls.

Because bookshops are among the very few places where one can spend time without spending any money, George Orwell noted, any number of practically certifiable lunatics are guaranteed to be regularly found in most of them.

I've finished that chapel I was painting. The Pope is quite satisfied.

Wrote Michelangelo to his father, after four years' effort—and with no further need to let fall brooms or lumber.

So impoverished was Linnaeus as a university student that the closest he could come to repairing worn-out shoes was to stuff the holes with paper.

The general acceptance that it was Antonello da Messina who taught Venice the Flemish method of painting with oils rather than with tempera.

Venice—and thus Italy.

More floggings than meals.

Haydn remembered from his childhood.

Trying to imagine E.M. Forster, who found *Ulysses* indecorous, at a London performance of Lenny Bruce—to which in fact he was once taken.

Trying to imagine the same for a time-transported Nathaniel Hawthorne—who during his first visit to Europe was even shocked at the profusion of naked statues.

January 22, 1945, Else Lasker-Schüler died on.

Raskolnikov. Minus the last two letters, the word translates as *dissenter.*

While the pseudonym *Gorky* means *the bitter.*

Fifty years after combat in World War I, David Jones could still be momentarily panicked by an unexpected explosive sound like that of a backfiring truck.

And now we three in Euston waiting-room.

Latin, Greek, Italian, and German, George Eliot read.

Latin, Greek, Italian, and French—Mary Shelley.

Hindi, not English, Rudyard Kipling's first language was.

People who pronounce the word *ask* as if it were spelled with an *x.*

As for that matter it was, until the late sixteenth century.

If God had not created breasts, I would not have become a painter.

Renoir once unseriously announced.

A woman's breast or a commonplace milk bottle—my feelings remained the same when painting either.

Corot soberly insisted.

Nobody comes. Nobody calls—

Which Novelist after a moment realizes may sound like a line of Beckett's, but is actually something he himself has said in an earlier book.

The name Copperfield came from a sign Dickens had noticed on a shop in a London slum.

Chuzzlewit likewise.

Nothing but obscenities and filth.

Being all Conrad could find in D.H. Lawrence.

Disgust and horror, recorded Abigail Adams after a blackface performance of *Othello:*

My whole soul shuddered whenever I saw the sooty heretic Moor touch the fair Desdemona.

The revolver with which van Gogh shot himself had been borrowed. Van Gogh having claimed he wished to fire at crows that were annoying him as he painted.

The first requirement for a composer is to be dead.

Said Arthur Honegger.

Remembering that before writing *Ben Hur,* Lew Wallace had been a Union general during the Civil War.

Remembering that Abner Doubleday had been the same.

The endless commentary, and analysis, and even retelling, in *Clarissa.* Anyone reading it just for the story would hang himself, Johnson said.

Is Moby Dick the whale or the man?

James Thurber said Harold Ross had to ask.

Roughly two-thirds of the paintings described in the corrected second edition of Vasari's *Lives* —finished in 1567—would appear to no longer exist.

Hamlet. A boring play full of quotations.

Swinburne's delirium-tremendous imagination, Hopkins called it.

Grant Wood's sister, Nan, and a dentist named McKeeby. Who posed for *American Gothic.*

In Cedar Rapids.

July 4, 1934, Hayyim Bialik died on.

The letter announcing the first acceptance of a poem by Francis Thompson never reached him.

Thompson being so indigent at the time that he literally had no address.

Poe, in his late thirties a half-century earlier—

Unable even to afford postage to put his manuscripts in the mail.

For poor people, sick or lame, or travelers.

Advertised the Savoy, a charitable residence in sixteenth-century London—which also saw fit to take in struggling authors.

Thinking of them for so long as essentially literary characters that one has to force oneself to recall that Dante actually *knew* the Paolo of Paolo and Francesca.

Goya died at eighty-three.

Having had to read lips for the last thirty-six years of his life.

Borges at eighty-six.

Having had to be read aloud to for almost as long.

Ovid's poem about his sweetheart Corinna's near-fatal abortion—dated ca. 23BC.

The child was mine—or so I at least do think.

Baudelaire's addiction to laudanum.

Coleridge's. De Quincey's.

Poe's.

The *Nike of Samothrace,* in the Louvre, which was excavated in 1863—in more than one hundred fragments.

Newspapers expressed such indignation over the ostensible immorality in Richard Strauss's *Salome* at its 1907 American premiere that the opera was withdrawn after a single performance and not produced again at the Metropolitan until 1934.

Diseased and polluted. Indescribably, yes, inconceivably, gross and abominable. Unspeakable.

Read a small portion of what the *New York Times* had to contribute.

Aristide Maillol's practice of repeatedly urinating on his bronze sculptures.

To add patina.

If you value my work, please, do not knock.

Requested a notice on Hermann Hesse's door in Ticino.

Gérard de Nerval, in some of the milder moments of his madness—known to toss such money as he possessed into the air for anyone's taking in restaurants and coffeehouses.

Anne Sexton's periods in mental institutions.

Only native-born citizens in ancient Athens were allowed to own property.

Meaning that no less a personage than Aristotle, from Stagira, could not.

The nunnery on Montmartre, mentioned a few years earlier by François Villon, where in 1503 it was discovered that the abbess and several nuns had borne children—and still others were pregnant.

A fiend of a book. The action is laid in Hell—only it seems places and people have English names there.

Said Dante Gabriel Rossetti of *Wuthering Heights.*

Olive Fremstad. Mary Garden. Ljuba Welitsch. Karita Matilla.

Wagner played the piano badly.

Berlioz not at all.

For safety's sake during the bombings of World War II, the Elgin Marbles were removed from the British Museum and stored deep in the London subway system.

While the French Resistance during those same years was using the Lascaux cave as a place in which to cache weapons.

Tchaikovsky was found weeping after he had written the death of Lisa in *The Queen of Spades.*

Georges Bernanos was married to a direct descendant of a brother of Joan of Arc.

A simple creature unlettyrde.

Julian of Norwich called herself.

The most unlearned and uninformed female who ever dared to be an authoress.

Echoed Jane Austen—four hundred years afterward.

Pastor Martin Niemöller—who spent seven years at Sachsenhausen and Dachau.

After having been a German U-boat commander in World War I.

April 13, 1945, Ernst Cassirer died on.

Ivan Goncharov worked in the Russian Civil Service for his entire adult life.

Mussorgsky, the same.

Then again, quoting himself or not, Novelist naturally does receive some few phone calls after all.

All too often in these years with news of someone's death, however.

Leonardo's peculiar habit of surreptitiously following interesting-looking strangers on the street.

To be able to sketch them from memory later, the contemporary assumption was.

Christianity must be divine, since it has lasted seventeen hundred years despite the fact of being so full of villainy and absurdity.

Voltaire said.

The first priest was the first rogue who crossed paths with the first fool.

Voltaire also said.

Slop, Pound was calling Yeats's recent verse in the mid-1930s—after having been best man at Yeats's wedding two decades earlier.

The influence of Donne upon the literature of England was singularly wide and deep—although almost wholly malign.

Said Edmund Gosse.

There is no indication whatsoever of anything even remotely resembling a State of Israel on the maps in most contemporary Arab schoolbooks.

Sixty-seven, Cézanne died at.

Some few days after having been caught for hours in a sudden downpour where he had been at work on a landscape.

A sort of God of painting.

Matisse was to call him.

One can now hear famous pieces of music as easily as one can buy a glass of beer.

Proclaimed Debussy in delight at the advent of the phonograph.

They who drink beer will think beer.

Said Washington Irving.

Cracked, Edith Sitwell called Blake.

Flaubert's outrage at the notion of an illustrated edition of *Bovary.*

Jane, Jane,
Tall as a crane,
The morning light creaks down again.

Still the most avant-garde book ever written.

Anthony Burgess said of *Tristram Shandy.*

A man is in general better pleased when he has a good dinner upon his table, than when his wife talks Greek.

Johnson said.

Mahler died in 1911. Alma not until 1964.

Beckett, on the posthumous publication of letters or other papers that their authors might not have approved of:

When a writer dies his widow should be burned on his funeral pyre.

To publish one line of an author which he himself did not intend for publication—especially letters—is a despicable act.

Had said Heine earlier.

What the dickens, lower case—which has nothing to do with the author of *Great Expectations.*

I cannot tell what the dickens his name is, says someone in *The Merry Wives of Windsor,* on stage by 1601.

It is never difficult to paint, said Dalí.

It is either easy or impossible.

Willie Yeats, he was frequently called.

William Cuthbert Faulkner, his full name was.

Christopher Marlowe evidently wrote *Tamburlaine* while still a student at Cambridge.

Learn or leave. A third alternative is to be flogged.

Declared a Latin inscription at the entrance to a church-sponsored Medieval English elementary school.

Rousseau's father was a watchmaker.

Lady Mary Wortley Montagu died of breast cancer.

Too much interest in music could turn one effeminate.

Kant said.

Tolstoy's certainty that Darwin was already beginning to be forgotten.

As early as in 1903.

Hugh Kenner's sense of the same *re* Freud.

Whom he called already nearly as dated as *Trilby* —in 1958.

Goyisher kopf.

Byron, with amiable confidence, to friends whose silence suggested that they did not particularly admire *Don Juan:*

I wish you all better taste.

The ugliness of some of his music is really masterly.

Stated a London journal after an early Delius concert.

Andromache. Alcestis. Helen. Medea. The Bacchae.

Each of which Euripides ends with his chorus speaking an *identical* verse—to the effect that the ways of the gods are unpredictable.

Helen, the most famous woman in Greek mythology—whose name is not a Greek name.

The curiosity that we possess copies of ten evidently authentic letters of Dante's—and not one of Shakespeare's.

August 11, 1494, Hans Memling died on.

Dylan Thomas's eighteenth birthday, Sylvia Plath was born on.

I hate that dreadful hollow behind the little wood.

Strolling on Park Avenue in New York, John Gielgud unexpectedly runs into Greta Garbo—

Looking like a displaced charwoman, he later reports.

Edgell Rickword lost an eye as an officer in France in World War I.

Siegfried Sassoon was wounded twice.

Thinking with someone else's brain.

Schopenhauer called reading.

In the late spring of 1944, at the height of their efficiency, the forty-six ovens in the crematoriums at Auschwitz were incinerating as many as twelve thousand corpses per day.

The word *genocide* had not existed until being coined by a Polish scholar in that same year.

Italo Svevo had to pay to publish *Confessions of Zeno.*

Stratford-on-Avon, Marie Corelli died in.

I say that if you can tell a story in a picture and if a reasonable number of people like your work, it is art.

Said Norman Rockwell.

If more than ten percent of the population likes a painting it should be burned.

Said Shaw.

Ronald Reagan was a clandestine informer for the FBI when it was investigating so-called left-wing influences in Hollywood in the 1940s.

Confucius was illegitimate.

Michelangelo's passing comment to Raphael, at the Vatican, that there was a young painter in Florence who would bring sweat to his brow—unquote—if he ever fulfilled himself.

Meaning Andrea del Sarto.

Michelangelo, who was incidentally eight years older than Raphael—and would outlive him by forty-four.

And Andrea by thirty-three.

The paper shit is endless.

Quoth a 1911 letter of Einstein's *re* university teaching.

Reviewers who have accused Novelist of inventing some of his anecdotes and/or quotations—without the elemental responsibility to do the checking that would verify every one of them.

Asking a working writer what he thinks about critics is like asking a lamppost what it feels about dogs.

Said John Osborne.

Sein oder nicht sein—ja, dass ist die Frage.

Reads Schlegel's translation.

March 3, 1996, Marguerite Duras died on.

Simonides once rejected a meager fee to compose an ode to the winner of a mule race, insisting he did not write about jackasses.

The fee was increased. *Wind-swift steeds,* the jackasses miraculously became.

Isamu Noguchi's sets for Martha Graham.

Eva Hesse was dead at thirty-four.

The fact is, I did not eat every day during that period of my life.

Said André Breton, explaining a possible origin for some of his earliest surrealist writings.

The Pope may judge all and be judged by no man.

Said Innocent III.

Pericles' mistress Aspasia, who ran a school for courtesans—and was comfortably at home in intellectual discussion with Socrates.

No different than what happens at the Skull and Bones initiation.

Said someone on radio named Rush Limbaugh about American soldiers abusing prisoners at Abu Ghraib in Iraq.

People having a good time.

Bovine spongiform encephalopathy.

On exhibition in a New York gallery in 2005, a portrait of Seamus Heaney—by Derek Walcott.

Which would barely pass muster in an undergraduate painting class, according to the *New York Times.*

Curiously impressed by the fact that Auden paid every one of his bills—electric, phone, whatever—on the same day that it arrived.

Boccaccio, one of the few intellectuals in the late Middle Ages determined to recover ancient manuscripts—but all too often coming upon them in monastery storerooms never locked, with pages torn out by the fistful, with what remains refuse-strewn and indecipherable. At Monte Cassino grass even grows in the loft where windows stand open.

Boccaccio bursts into tears.

Cavafy was forty-one before his first book was published—containing fourteen poems.

Remembering that in the *Iliad,* as rife with detailed violence as any war narrative ever written, not one captured Greek or Trojan is ever tortured.

—And that the only Southerner hanged by the Union during the Civil War was the commanding officer at Andersonville—where inconceivably barbarous conditions had cost 12,000 incarcerated Northerners their lives.

Teaching at New York University before its graduate art program had been fully established, during Prohibition, Erwin Panofsky sometimes met with students at a Fifty-Second Street speakeasy.

Juvenile trash.

Edmund Wilson dismissed the sum of J.R.R. Tolkien as.

Alicia Markova almost never in her career weighed more than ninety-eight pounds.

Was it Brigid Brophy who gave up on a certain Virginia Woolf novel when she discovered that Woolf believed one needed a corkscrew to open a bottle of champagne?

February 25, 1547, Vittoria Collona died on.

The first time that Ethel Waters sang *Stormy Weather,* in a show at the Cotton Club, she was given no fewer than twelve encores.

A Metropolitan Opera audience once demanded so many curtain calls after a Renata Tebaldi Desdemona that she finally came back out with her coat and hat on.

All the fruit will fall from any tree beneath which a menstruating woman happens to sit.

Says Pliny's *Natural History.*

While also announcing that women who sneeze after making love are almost certain to miscarry.

The film *Carmen Jones,* with Dorothy Dandridge.

In which the dubbed lyric soprano voice is that of a very young Marilyn Horne.

The 1915 Cecil B. DeMille film of *Carmen* itself, with Geraldine Farrar.

Silent.

Stephen Crane was officially cited for bravery while a foreign correspondent during the Spanish-American War. At Guantánamo.

Will no one free me of this turbulent priest?

Canterbury, Joseph Conrad is buried in.

The only exercise I get these days is walking behind the coffins of my friends who took exercise.

Said Peter O'Toole in his late sixties.

Karl Marx regularly read Shakespeare aloud to his young children.

A scheme of Robert Boyle's, roughly 330 years ago, as recounted in Aubrey's *Brief Lives:*

At his owne costs and chardges, he gott translated and printed the New Testament into Arabique, to send into the Mahometan countreys.

Every word of importance is already in the Koran. Anything in any other books can only be pernicious.

Having been the Muslim rationalization for destroying all 700,000 volumes in the great library at Alexandria in 642.

Is T.S. Eliot the only poet one can think of who could have spent a year on his own in Paris at twenty-three—and managed to have no sexual encounters whatever?

You have but two topics, yourself and me, and I'm sick of both.

Johnson once told Boswell.

I come of a people who do not even acknowledge Jesus Christ. Why am I supposed to acknowledge Abstract Expressionism?

Asked Jack Levine.

The porphyry disc near the center of the Piazza della Signoria in Florence, marking the spot where Savonarola was burned at the stake in 1498.

The statue of Giordano Bruno on the spot in the Piazza Campo de' Fiori, in Rome, where he was burned in 1600.

Not distinguished looking in any way—neither handsome nor ugly, neither fat nor thin, neither tall nor short.

Said George Eliot of Dickens.

A peculiar face—not handsome, very ugly indeed.

Said Charlotte Brontë—of Thackeray.

No course in Shakespeare was taught at Harvard until as late as the 1870s.

Quentin de La Tour, harmlessly deranged in his later years—and frequently seen talking to trees.

Another of Novelist's economic-status epiphanies:

Walking four or five blocks out of his way, and back, to save little more than nickels on some common household item.

While needing to stop to rest at least two or three times en route.

Writers are the beggars of Western society.

Said Octavio Paz.

There is no way of being a creative writer in America without being a loser.

Said Nelson Algren.

Finding oneself momentarily startled by a reference in Gorky's diaries to Tolstoy chatting with Chekhov.

On the telephone.

Thou shalt not be afraid for the terror by night.

Says the King James translation of Psalms 91:5.

Thou shalt not nede to be afrayed for eny bugges by night.

Says Miles Coverdale's earlier version.

A designated area for booksellers existed in the central market in Athens as far back as in the fifth century BC.

The report from that same era to the effect that Aeschylus gave up writing after members of an audience were killed when a tier of wooden benches collapsed during a performance of his work.

At least one of Modigliani's sculptures was carved from a discarded construction-site stone—because he could not afford to pay money for something better.

Jean-Baptiste Lully's confessor once refused to grant him absolution unless Lully agreed to destroy the score of a recent opera, which the confessor believed blasphemous. Lully let the work be burned and was properly shrived.

With an extra copy safely set aside.

Neither Graham Greene nor Evelyn Waugh ever learned to drive a car.

I always said God was against art and I still believe it.

Said Edward Elgar—while impatiently awaiting acclaim.

All artists are bores.

Unquote. Clement Greenberg.

By the sentence of the angels, by the decree of the saints, we anathematize, execrate, curse, and cast out Baruch Spinoza, the whole of the sacred community assenting—

This trivial and vulgar way of union; it is the foolishest act a wise man commits in all his life.

Declaimed Sir Thomas Browne—about sex.

Organized Christian denominations and their individual congregations:

Chain stores and their retail outlets, Thorstein Veblen called them.

Duke Ellington and Miles Davis are buried in the same Bronx cemetery.

Chopin was buried in Père Lachaise in Paris—but with Polish earth later sprinkled on the grave.

—There shall be no man speak to him, no man write to him, no man show him any kindness, no man stay under the same roof with him, no man come nigh him.

The greatest novel ever written.

Kingsley called *Uncle Tom's Cabin.*

It was a bright cold day in April, and the clocks were striking thirteen.

November 6 or 7, 1944, Hannah Senesch was executed on.

As his once extraordinary fame in France's literary world faded, Chateaubriand also became extremely hard of hearing.

He only thinks he is deaf because he no longer hears himself talked about, Talleyrand said.

Virgil was five years older than Horace.

Wondering when and where the last casual streetcorner conversation in Latin might have taken place.

Norma loquendi.

The rumor that Frieda Lawrence's lover after Lawrence's death, whom she asked to transport Lawrence's ashes from France to New Mexico, indifferently dumped them—and substituted no one knows what before the Taos reburial.

Mouse-poor, Robert Graves describes John Clare as having been.

Drunk as a mouse.

Chaucer somewhere writes.

A sub-human species without any of the cultural or social refinements of our time.

General George S. Patton compassionately described Jewish concentration-camp survivors as.

Picasso. Cézanne. Matisse. Braque. Bonnard. Renoir.

All of whom painted portraits of Ambroise Vollard.

Cartier-Bresson. Brassaï. Man Ray. Lee Miller. Robert Doisneau. Robert Capa. David Douglas Duncan. Cecil Beaton.

All of whom photographed Picasso.

George Washington's will called for the freeing of his slaves.

As had Aristotle's for the freeing of most of his—2,100 years earlier.

More's *Utopia,* in which women are granted full and equal rights to education with men—dated 1516.

Pulmonary fibrosis, Marlon Brando died of.

Don't keep talking to me about nature, said Corot. All I see out there are Corots.

A 1940 letter from Béla Bartók, new in New York, about attempting to go by subway from Forest Hills, in Queens, to lower Manhattan—

And spending three mystified hours underground before sneaking shamefacedly home—his words—without ever achieving his destination.

Turner's eternal stovepipe hat.

Eliot's bowler.

Saul Bellow's fedora.

A precious, priestly, hothouse darling.

Sir Arthur Quiller-Couch dismissed Hopkins as.

Revolting, the *London Times* called Millais' *Christ in the House of His Parents.*

The occasion, soon after Vladimir Horowitz became Toscanini's son-in-law, on which Toscanini leaned from the podium and patted him on the head at the end of a performance.

Green eyes, the self-portraits indicate van Gogh had.

It has been possible for a long time to conceive of a poet who has never written a poem.

Leslie Fiedler once said.

Debussy never learned which side won World War I.

Old enough to have started coming upon likenesses on postage stamps of other writers he had known personally or had at least met in passing.

Anthony Trollope was once told by an acquaintance that one of his recurring serialized characters had become boring.

Trollope killed her off in the next installment.

The misfortunate, otherwise unknown first-century BC Roman Egnatius—remembered because of a poem in which Catullus accuses him of cleaning his teeth with urine.

The only excuse for the suffering that God allows in the world—is that he does not exist.

Stendhal said.

Elizabeth Barrett Browning's addiction to morphine.

And/or ether.

Is there one major Dostoievsky novel in which no one commits suicide?

Dostoievsky gave me more than any thinker, more even than Gauss.

Einstein said.

Former Naval Person—

Winston Churchill's code name having been in World War II.

Colonel Berger—

Malraux's, in the Resistance.

Kipling, who was forty-two, remains the youngest author to win the Nobel Prize.

Camus was forty-four.

July 17, 1967, John Coltrane died on.

Aspen, Colorado, Mina Loy died in.

Thomas Hardy's first wife, Emma, kept a twenty-year diary that was evidently devoted almost entirely to the evisceration of his character.

Hardy burned every word of it at her death.

A second wife, Florence, once accused him of not having spoken to anyone outside of their house in twelve days. Hardy insisted he had.

He had said good morning to the manure-cart driver.

O body, mass of corruptions, what have I to do with thee?

Asked Augustine.

The proper study of mankind is books.

Said Aldous Huxley.

Benoit Mandelbrot.

Benoit de Sainte-Maure.

Émile Zola's certainty that after a hundred years *Les Fleurs du Mal* would be no more than a footnoted curiosity in literary history.

Maugham's—that there was nothing to be found in Mallarmé but pretense and platitudes.

The identity of the Immortal Beloved.

Keep hold of my arm, they must make room for us, not we for them.

Shortly after its publication, Robert McAlmon informed Joyce that he planned to throw his copy of *Ulysses* out the window. Joyce told him not to:

Socrates might be passing in the street.

E.M. Forster never gets any further than warming the teapot.

Said Katherine Mansfield.

The early Shakespearean Betterton, distressed over foreign intrusions onto the late seventeenth-century London stage:

By squeaking Italians and capering monsieurs, end quote.

Shakespeare's birthday, Turner was born on.

More greatness in this man than in any other born in our times.

Vasari saw in Donatello.

What needs to be said is best said twice.

Said Empedocles.

At one point near the end of the Reign of Terror, more than 1,300 guillotined prisoners were flung into the same single Paris mass grave—one of the 1,300 having been André Chénier.

Continued speculation that Abraham Lincoln was homosexual.

Bologna, Lodovico Carracci died in.

Parma, Agostino.

Rome, Annibale.

Theodore Dreiser's general preference for the word *kike,* rather than Jew.

If it were up to me, I would have wiped my behind with his last decree.

Said Mozart—after a demand by the Archbishop of Salzburg for more brevity in his church compositions.

Fish feel pain.

A seminonfictional semifiction.

And with its interspersed unattributed quotations at roughest count adding up to a hundred or more.

Good lord, Willie, you are drunk. Either that or you're writing for a very small audience.

Is Sir Walter Raleigh and his cloak the oldest tale from English history that children still remember?

Or King Alfred and the cakes?

'Tis such a task as scarce leaves a man time to be a good neighbour, an useful friend, nay, to plant a tree, much less to save his soul.

Said Pope, *re* writing well.

Michelangelo's *Pietà—*

Is the Virgin many years too young?

Dante will always remain popular because nobody ever reads him.

Said Voltaire.

Approximately seventy-five years before Blake learned Italian to do so—at sixty.

The cocktail party at Peggy Guggenheim's Manhattan townhouse during which Jackson Pollock casually urinated into the fireplace.

At more than nine thousand published pages, does Karl Barth's *Church Dogmatics* have any competition as the longest *unfinished* book of the twentieth century?

Is I Samuel 18:20, where it is stated that King Saul's daughter Michal loves David, the only place in the Old Testament where a woman is reported to actually love a man?

Even if by II Samuel 6:16 we find her learning to despise him?

The paintings of a drunken privy cleaner.

A Cézanne critic spoke of.

The two younger brothers of William and Henry James—both of whom were wounded while fighting for the Union during the Civil War.

I have never been surprised to find men wicked, but I have often been surprised to find them not ashamed.

Said Swift.

Even though they had dedicated poems to each other, because of the conditions of life in Russia Anna Akhmatova and Marina Tsvetayeva managed to meet only once—little more than a year before Tsvetayeva would hang herself.

Gaiety is the most outstanding feature of the Soviet Union.

Stalin once actually ventured.

No girl was ever seduced by a book.

Postulated Jimmy Walker.

Briseis, in the *Iliad,* who is not identified at all except as the captive maiden taken by Agamemnon from Achilles.

But who over the centuries is transformed into the Cressida of Chaucer and Shakespeare.

And whose name is in fact not a name—but means only the woman from Brisa, a town in Lesbos.

If the Republicans would stop telling lies about the Democrats, we would stop telling the truth about them.

Adlai Stevenson said.

It Ain't Necessarily So. In Danish.

Which was piped into Danish radio by the underground whenever announcements were made of German victories in World War II.

Baldur von Schirach, one of the chief Nazi war criminals tried at Nuremberg, on the origin of his anti-Semitism:

From a book about the Jews by Henry Ford.

The woman sleeping on the sofa dreams that she is transported into the forest, hearing the music of the snake charmer's instrument. This explains why the sofa is in the picture.

Unquote—Le Douanier.

Looking is not as simple as it looks.

Said Ad Reinhardt.

Eighty sopranos. Eighty contraltos. Seventy basses. Sixty tenors.

—Called for in Belioz' *Grande Messe des Mortes.*

Over the hill to the poorhouse
I'm trudgin' my weary way.

He is the handsomest man in England, and he wears the most beautiful shirts.

Said Yeats of Rupert Brooke.

If on a winter's night with no other source of warmth, Novelist were to burn an Andy Warhol, qualms?

Qualmless.

Jane Ellen Harrison was proficient in fourteen languages.

Utrillo, on the occasion of one of his several arrests for drunkenness—trying to commit suicide by smashing his head against the walls of his Montmartre jail cell.

Housman, in the early 1920s, *re* what may have been the first flight taken by an author:

The machine required repairs, having been damaged on the previous day by a passenger who butted his head through a window to be sick.

We should look upon the female state as being as it were a deformity, though one which occurs in the ordinary course of nature.

Determined Aristotle.

Brendan Behan, to a nun caring for him in a Catholic hospital:

Bless you, Sister. May all your sons be bishops.

Starting out, George Gershwin sold his first two songs for a total of twelve dollars.

October 24, 1725, Alessandro Scarlatti died on.

July 23, 1757, Domenico.

The curious theatrical superstition that insists it is unlucky to talk about *Macbeth* by name—the Scottish play, being how it is usually referred to instead.

King Lear's wife. Goneril's mother, Regan's, Cordelia's.

How often does it occur to anyone that there is not one remotest allusion to her in the text?

Gravesend, on the Thames, Pocahontas died in.

The last time anyone mentioned Sherwood Anderson.

There are so many ways of earning a living, and most of them are failures.

Wrote Gertrude Stein.

Alice B. Toklas did the cooking.

Moments in which Novelist does something like searching interminably at every hook and hanger in the apartment for his shirt—and only at the point of utter bewilderment realizing that he is wearing it.

Pushkin's beautiful seventeen-year-old wife Nathalie, whom he married at thirty-one—and whom he said was the one hundred and thirteenth woman he had been in love with.

As a student, Anna Netrebko scrubbed floors in a St. Petersburg opera house.

The word *agnostic.*

Coined by Thomas Henry Huxley during the early debates on Darwinism.

Norbert Wiener graduated from Tufts University at fourteen. And owned a Ph.D. from Harvard four years later.

Wonderful news—

Said meringue-brained Bobby Fischer at the destruction of the World Trade Center.

Did Toulouse-Lautrec die from a sequence of strokes—or from syphilitic paralysis?

1922. *Ulysses.*

1922. *The Waste Land.*

1922. *Reader's Digest.*

The first English novel for adults, Virginia Woolf called *Middlemarch.*

There are 773,692 words in the King James Bible.

Or 773,746.

The wastepaper basket is the author's best friend.

Noted Isaac Bashevis Singer.

Wondering by what date the last survivor of the Holocaust will have died.

You can be up to your boobies in white satin, with gardenias in your hair and no sugar cane for miles, but you can still be working on a plantation.

Said Billie Holiday.

I am not tragically colored. There is no great sorrow dammed up in my soul. I do not belong to that sobbing school of Negrohood who hold that nature somehow has given them a lowdown dirty deal.

Conversely offered Zora Neale Hurston.

Pietro Aretino died in the midst of a hysterical fit of laughter that apparently turned into an apoplectic stroke.

As had the Athenian comic playwright Philemon—at ninety-nine.

Or one hundred and one.

Lord Byron by the kilo, Dumas père described George Sand's early romantic novels as.

Renaissance paintings on which Bernard Berenson falsified the attributions—when handed money under the table by the dealer Duveen.

Jude the Obscene, someone called it.

As an apprentice, Claude Lorrain worked with the landscape painter Agostino Tassi—who a few years earlier had earned such small art-world immortality as he possesses by raping Artemisia Gentileschi.

Artemisia. Who is granted only one sentence in Novelist's two-volume 1962 *Everyman's Dictionary of Pictorial Art*—at the end of the entry on her father.

All female artists are sluts.

Quoth Flaubert's *Dictionary of Accepted Ideas.*

I leave before being left. I decide.

Said Brigitte Bardot.

Winslow Homer spent his last twenty-seven years on the isolated Maine peninsula of Prout's Neck.

—My nearest neighbor is half a mile away. I am four miles from the PO and under a snowbank most of the time. Night before last it was twelve below zero.

January 13, 1864, Stephen Foster died on.

Little Friend, Little Friend, I got two engines on fire. Can you see me, Little Friend?

I'm crossing right over you. Let's go home.

Guido Reni's abnormally exaggerated terror of witchcraft.

To the extent that the mere sight of an old woman at a market could send him rushing away.

Losing her sight in later life, Constance Garnett arranged to have Russian books read aloud—and then *dictated* her translations.

A quack, Vladimir Nabokov called Thomas Mann.

A complete mediocrity—D.H. Lawrence.

That total fake—Ezra Pound.

Despicable, loathsome, sick, third-rate—Dostoievsky.

Time is the only critic without ambition.

John Steinbeck said.

The severest test of the imagination—is to name a cat.

Said Samuel Butler.

Schopenhauer's poodle.

Called Atma.

Picasso's play, *Desire Caught by the Tail*—which could be performed for the first time only privately, because of the Nazi occupation of Paris.

But *avec* Camus, Sartre, Michel Leiris, Raymond Queneau, Dora Maar, Pierre Reverdy, Simone de Beauvoir.

The short story by one Heinz von Lichberg, published in Berlin six years before Nabokov would live there for a decade and a half—about an older man's obsession with a young girl.

—And entitled *Lolita.*

There are four chances in 2,598,960 of being dealt a royal flush in a hand of poker.

How old would you be if you didn't know how old you was?

Asked Satchel Paige.

Baudelaire wrote a poem about Watteau.

Verlaine wrote a poem about Watteau.

Proust wrote a poem about Watteau.

The Protocols of the Elders of Zion, long since categorically exposed as a fraud.

Nonetheless incessantly reprinted throughout the Muslim world—not to add dramatized on television.

Kant's father was a saddle maker.

If you are going to make a book end badly, Robert Louis Stevenson once pointed out, it must end badly from the beginning—

Such as by mentioning an eighth-story roof in its very first paragraphs.

And which should presumably call to mind Chekhov's admonition that if a pistol is displayed in a first act, it had damned well better be fired by the last.

Raphael died on his thirty-seventh birthday.

Always young in men's memories, someone thought to say.

Old. Tired. Sick. Alone. Broke.

Only days before Edna St. Vincent Millay's birth, her mother's brother's life was saved in a New York hospital. Millay's middle name, those few days later, was taken from the name of the hospital.

Florence Nightingale.

Simply because she was born there.

Canon in D Major for Strings and Continuo.

By Johann Pachelbel.

Does having been six feet eight inches tall make Charles Olson the tallest known poet?

How tall was William Langland, who because of his height was called Long Will?

One half of the children born die before their eighth year. This is nature's law; why try to contradict it?

Inquired Rousseau.

John Jay Chapman's conclusion that a visiting Martian would come away with a more critical lesson about life on earth from attending an Italian opera than from reading Emerson.

The lesson that there are two sexes.

September 13, 1506, Andrea Mantegna died on.

Kenesaw Mountain Landis.

Lente currite noctis equi.

Says Ovid in the *Amores.*

O lente lente currite noctis equi.

Says Marlowe, at the end of *Faustus.*

Of no significance whatsoever. But the hospital where Dylan Thomas would die, sixty-one years after the fact, was the one after which Edna Millay had been named.

O run slowly, slowly, horses of the night.

Pandora's box. Which in the first written version of the tale, in Hesiod, is in fact a jar.

A reference to the good old hearty female stench, unquote.

Which Pound excised from Eliot's manuscript of *The Waste Land.*

Sacred Scripture tells us that Joshua commanded the sun to stand still, not the earth.

Said Luther, dismissing *this fool,* Copernicus.

Flat, clumsy, labored, and embarrassingly crude, Isaac Deutscher called *Doctor Zhivago.*

Which Akhmatova found so intermittently inept that she refused to believe Pasternak had written it all.

Like Benedetto Croce earlier, Ignazio Silone lost both of his parents in an earthquake.

Paul Robeson's *Othello.*

With José Ferrer as Iago.

Renée Fleming's Metropolitan opening-night Desdemona—sung only three weeks after having given birth to a second child.

Because of a promise to his mother, Jorge Luis Borges recited the Lord's Prayer every night of his life:

Even though I don't know whether there's anybody at the other end of the line.

God seems to have left the receiver off the hook.

Once suggested Arthur Koestler—in more general political terms.

And prayers have no power the Plague to stay.

Wrote Long Will.

Montaigne was taught to read and speak Latin before he knew French.

Sor Juana Inés de la Cruz was reading Plato and Aristophanes, in Latin translations, at the age of eight.

Anton Bruckner, in old age, tells Gustav Mahler that he can readily foresee his coming interrogation by his Maker—

Why else have I given you talent, you son of a bitch, than that you should sing My praise and glory? But you have accomplished much too little.

Cosima Wagner's Jewish great-grandmother.

Egon Schiele was once briefly jailed—but then not prosecuted—on allegations of abducting and molesting a girl of thirteen.

Q. Who is the Buddha?

A. Three pounds of flax.

After a performance, Queen Victoria once ventured to inform Paderewski that he was a genius.

To which: Perhaps, Your Majesty. But before that I was a drudge.

The word *nihilism.*

Coined by Turgenev, for use in *Fathers and Sons.*

The next night he did not know where he was, did not feel the cold. The wind blew dust along the ground and into his mouth as he sang.

Nelson, at Trafalgar. Who had a horseshoe nailed to the mainmast of the *Victory* before the battle.

Niels Bohr—who kept one above a door in his vacation home.

Niels Bohr.

I would rather have a drop of luck than a barrel of brains.

Allegedly said Diogenes.

Franco Zeffirelli's *Taming of the Shrew.* In which Zeffirelli's name in the credits was larger than Shakespeare's.

Please return this book. I find that though many of my friends are poor mathematicians, they are nearly all good bookkeepers.

Read Walter Scott's bookplate.

January 14, 2005, Victoria de los Angeles died on.

Ivor Gurney, who was both wounded and gassed at Passchendaele, spent the last fifteen of his remaining twenty years in a mental institution—convinced that the war was still going on.

Italo Calvino died after a cerebral hemorrhage suffered while sitting in a garden.

A portable fatherland, Heine called the Torah.

From a letter of Petrarch's, ca. 1352, in which he mentions having been reminded of some task or other by the town clock:

By this recent invention we now measure time in almost all of the cities of northern Italy.

Eliot's second marriage, in 1957, took place in the same Kensington church where Jules Laforgue had been married seventy-one years earlier—which Eliot claimed not to have known beforehand.

How can 59,054,087 People Be So Dumb?

Asked the principal headline in the *London Daily Mirror* after the reelection of George W. Bush in 2004.

G.E. Moore was known to appear at his Cambridge classroom in bedroom slippers.

Father, dear father, come home with me now!
The clock in the steeple strikes one.

I don't go upstairs two nights out of seven without taking Washington Irving under my arm.

Said Dickens.

Actually, the door to Novelist's roof is connected to an alarm. Workmen unable to locate the building superintendent now and again trip it. No one pays any attention, however.

Jean Giraudoux spent two very brief periods, when young, as an instructor at Harvard.

And for years thereafter kept a Harvard pennant above the bed in his Paris apartment.

The writer Bret Easton Ellis, who imparted to a *New York Times* reporter that he had been reading the Bible—but then seemed uncertain as to whether in the Old Testament or the New.

Were the stories about Moses or Jesus?

Jesus. I think.

The frequent blind beggars in Euripides, particularly in plays now lost.

The crutch and cripple playwright, Aristophanes called him.

August Strindberg's mother had been a barmaid.

The marriage of Roberta Peters and Robert Merrill—which lasted three months.

The Greatest Novel Reader in the World.

Elizabeth Barrett Browning suggested her own epitaph could well be.

Jean-Michel Basquiat died of a heroin overdose. At twenty-seven. Sir Thomas Bodley, who organized the Oxford library subsequently named the Bodleian, permitted the inclusion of no such idle bookes and riffe raffes—unquote—as writings for the current theater.

Including of course those of his almost exact contemporary Shakespeare.

Allen Ginsberg's insistence that he was once accosted by the apparitional voice of William Blake—immediately after masturbating.

How now! Whose mare's dead?

The extraordinary fame of Menander in antiquity—to the point where he is even quoted by Saint Paul.

Robert Graves' claim that as an infant at Wimbledon he had been occasionally patted on the head by Swinburne—he himself being wheeled by his nurse, Swinburne en route to his pub.

Theodore Watts-Dunton's wife's claim that when the monumentally alcoholic Swinburne was finally weaned away from brandy, he initially drank port because Tennyson did, then burgundy because of the Musketeers in Dumas, and at last ale—because of Shakespeare.

What a pleasant party, Plutarch records someone commenting to Timon of Athens.

It would be, if you were gone, Timon responds.

If there is anyone here I have forgotten to insult, I apologize.

Announced Brahms, exiting somewhere—2,300 years later.

Paul, thou art beside thyself; much learning doth make thee mad.

No battleship has yet been sunk by bombs.

Said the caption on a photograph of the USS *Arizona* in the program for the 1941 Army-Navy football game—eight days before Pearl Harbor.

Ovid's banishment from Rome by Augustus—which meant that his books were automatically removed from the city's libraries as well.

The similar banning of Virgil's and Livy's three decades later—by Caligula, who simply did not like them.

May the devil bung a cesspool with his skull.

Requested John Millington Synge, *re* a dim-witted reviewer.

One of us was once in love for eight days with a woman of fairly easy virtue, and the other for three days with a ten-franc whore. Altogether, eleven days of love between the two of us.

Being Edmond and Jules Goncourt, elucidating their relationships with the opposite sex.

Longfellow published his first poem at thirteen.

Bryant wrote *Thanatopsis* at seventeen—and after publication several years later was to hear it called a hoax.

No one, on this side of the Atlantic, is capable of writing such verses, insisted Richard Henry Dana.

Never having realized that there originally once was an actual troublemaking Irish family named Hooligan.

Or a military officer named Shrapnel.

The John Cage composition entitled *4'33"*.

In which the performer sits at a piano for four minutes and thirty-three seconds—and plays nothing.

Cervantes was fifty-eight when Part I of *Don Quixote* was published.

And sixty-eight at Part II.

Finding the earliest hints of a theory of evolution in Anaximander.

In the sixth century BC.

I never knew a writer's wife who wasn't beautiful.

Said Kurt Vonnegut.

Has Novelist ever known many who could not contrive some way to keep the pot boiling during fallow stretches?

General Mikhail T. Kalashnikov.

Joseph Ignace Guillotin.

Sir Rudolf Bing was once robbed of a cheap watch he wore only for sentimental reasons. Zinka Milanov was infuriated:

The General Manager of the Metropolitan Opera does not display a twenty-dollar wristwatch!

The mugging in which Giuseppe di Stefano, at eighty-three, was quite badly injured—while being stripped of a gold chain he had been given by Maria Callas.

It was Beckett's wife who took the call informing them that Beckett had won the Nobel Prize. Her first reaction, even as she turned to tell him:

Quelle catastrophe!

Toledo, Judah Halevi was born in.

Córdoba, Maimonides.

Saint Benedict, essentially the founder of moderate monastic rule.

Whose earliest regulations as an abbot were so harsh that the monks tried to poison his wine.

In the dense mist

What is being shouted

Between hill and boat?

Beethoven's brief period as a pupil of Hadyn's:
I never learned anything from the man.
There is no such thing as abstract art, said Picas-
so.
You always have to start somewhere or other.
Inconceivable nonsense.
Tchaikovsky called *Das Rheingold.*
Machiavelli's interminable visits to prostitutes—de-
scribed in unexpurgated detail in his correspondence.
Graham Greene's—so compulsive that a biographer
was able to reproduce a cryptic list, in Greene's
handwriting, of a favorite forty-seven.
Georges Simenon's—whose autobiography speaks
of as many as a thousand.
That man has missed something who has never
left a brothel at sunrise feeling like throwing himself
into the river out of pure disgust.
Says a Flaubert letter.
Yeats evidently knew no music.
The word *serendipity.*
Coined by Horace Walpole, in a 1754 fairy story.
August 22, 1904, Kate Chopin died on.
August 17, 1935, Charlotte Perkins Gilman.

George Eliot's instantaneous anger over any sort of anti-Semitic reference or joke.

Molière was on stage, performing in the role of the hypochondriac in his own last play *Le Malade imaginaire,* when he was stricken by the bursting blood vessel that caused his death a day later.

I hope I never get so old I get religious.

Quoth Ingmar Bergman.

Reviewers who protest that Novelist has lately appeared to be writing the same book over and over.

Like their grandly perspicacious uncles—who groused that Monet had done those damnable water lilies nine dozen times already also.

When a head and a book collide, and one sounds hollow—is it always the book?

Asked Lichtenberg.

Owls and cuckoos, asses, apes, and dogs.

Milton labeled critics.

Ménière's disease, Swift suffered from.

Erysipelas, Herman Melville.

Chopin's phthisis—which left him weighing less than one hundred pounds.

They told me I was everything; 'tis a lie—I am not ague-proof.

Realizes Lear.

The central railway-station platform of destinies.

Blaise Cendrars called early twentieth-century Bohemian Paris.

Virginia Woolf's suicide, for which she filled her pockets with stones before walking into the Ouse.

Wondering if anyone has ever noted how many stones—and what they might possibly have weighed?

Sleet falling;

Fathomless, infinite

Loneliness.

Verlaine was at most eight or nine feet away when he famously fired three shots at Rimbaud with a revolver—fortunately no more than wounding him in the wrist with the first and missing completely with the next two.

The painter of painters.

Manet called Velazquez.

A German equivalent of *Tubby,* Schubert's nickname was, among his friends.

Not to be born is far best.

Wrote Sophocles.

Not to be born at all would be the best thing.

Wrote Theognis, at least a half-century earlier.

Richard Feynman's conviction that as the perspective grows more and more distant, James Clerk Maxwell will loom ever larger as the single towering eminence of the nineteenth century.

The one truly great political figure of our age.

Einstein called Gandhi.

Dostoievsky's graduation from an engineering institute.

Achieved only after having first failed elementary algebra.

A cobbler makes a greater contribution to society than does a Homer or a Plato.

Asserted Proudhon.

Katherine Mansfield was dead at thirty-five.

March 7, 1944, Emmanuel Ringelbaum died on.

Ballplayers on the road live together. It won't work.

Said Rogers Hornsby *re* the signing of Jackie Robinson.

I only wished to tell people honestly: Look at yourselves, see how badly and boringly you live!

Said Chekhov, late along.

Tirso de Molina, who wrote the first dramatic version of the Don Juan legend—in which he allows someone to ask the stone Commendatore if there are taverns in the underworld.

And can poets down there still win prizes?

John Ruskin's insistence that he could never live in America—a country so miserable as to possess no castles, as he put it.

Freud's addiction to cocaine.

Sherlock Holmes'.

Contemporary college students—college students—who when asked to identify Joan of Arc have supposed her to be a character in the Biblical story of Noah and the flood.

Or indeed Noah's wife.

The first hospital in Europe was opened in Paris in the seventh century AD.

At least four hundred years after such things existed in Hindu India.

Last night I dreamt I went to Manderley again.

America is now given over to a damned mob of scribbling women.

Determined Hawthorne, in 1855.

The greatest achievement for a woman is to be as seldom as possible spoken of, said Thucydides.

Who mentions not one of them in his history.

Johnson's *Lives of the Poets*—which mentions none either.

Yasser Arafat was reported not to have read one book in the last forty years of his life.

But to have spent innumerable hours enrapt by Tom and Jerry cartoons.

The man who has seen a truly beautiful woman has seen God.

Said Rumi.

a pretty girl who naked is
is worth a million statues

Blaenau Ffestiniog, Gwynedd, John Cowper Powys died in.

By her own count, Vigée-Lebrun produced six hundred and sixty-two portraits.

Like many fond parents, I have in my heart of hearts a favourite child. And his name is David Copperfield.

Wrote Dickens.

Butterfly, my child.

Puccini spoke of her as.

William Faulkner. Seated on a park bench near City Hall in today's Oxford, Mississippi—in bronze.

Thomas Eakins was once accused of incest with a sister.

And a niece.

Henry Roth *acknowledged* the same with a sister—and for over a period of years.

Contemplating several of Turner's early watercolors, a prospective buyer implies that he has recently seen better.

Which has to mean you've been looking at Tom Girtin, Turner tells him.

Wondering if there can be any other ranking twentieth-century American poet whose body of work contains even half the percentage of pure *drivel* as Wallace Stevens'.

Novelist's calendar, which he leafs through idly to verify something he already suspected—that he has been out to dinner a grand total of three times in the entire past year, and then only when taken by some book person with an expense account.

The unceasing preoccupation with marriageableness and/or the economics of same in Jane Austen.

Suicide is more respectable, Emerson said.

Rarely remembering that the first translation from ancient Greek any of us learn to quote is of Pythagoras.

Kierkegaard's mother had originally been the family maid, whom his father married after the death of an earlier wife. There is not one word about her in anything Kierkegaard ever wrote, his journals included.

Henry Fielding's wife's maid—whom he likewise married after the wife's death.

Rembrandt's—who became his mistress.

Handel spent almost fifty years in London—and to the end spoke only broken English.

The square of the hypotenuse of a right triangle is equal to the sum of the et cetera.

Hideous, Hume condemned much of Spinoza as.

Anything that is too stupid to be spoken is sung.

Said Voltaire—describing opera.

Unlike most Italians, Joe DiMaggio never reeks of garlic.

Life magazine matter-of-factly took note of in 1939.

Not to add that he keeps his hair slick with water instead of olive oil or smelly bear grease—unquote, additionally.

And so to Mrs. Martin and there did what *je voudrais avec* her, both *devante* and backward.

Reads an entry in Samuel Pepys' diary for early June, 1666.

An earlier tenant in the same London building where Sylvia Plath would commit suicide—had been Yeats.

Pelion and Ossa. In *Odyssey* XI. In *Georgics* I. In Horace's *Odes* III.

With small Latin and less Greek, Shakespeare found them for *Hamlet* where?

The thirteen extant letters of Plato.

Did Plato write any of the thirteen?

Gertrude Stein once delighted Picasso by reporting that a collector had been dumbfounded, years afterward, to hear that Picasso had given her her portrait as a gift, rather than asking payment.

Not understanding that that early in Picasso's career, the difference had been next to negligible.

I don't think anybody should write his autobiography until after he's dead.

Said Samuel Goldwyn.

One author pilfers the best of another.
And calls it tradition.

Says a fragment of Bacchylides, ca. 450BC.

Brooklyn, Leonard Bernstein is buried in.

February 22, 1913, Saussure died on.

Too lazy to copy down passages he thought he might later wish to quote, De Quincey often simply ripped them out of the book at hand.

Even when the book was someone else's.

A photo of Lillie Langtry, as Rosalind in *As You Like It,* taken in 1882.

How can Novelist have fallen in love with someone dead since 1929?

Henry James, addressing Joseph Conrad: *Mon cher confrère.*

Conrad, addressing James: *Mon cher maître.*

Both, *repeatedly,* when in conversation, said Ford Madox Ford.

More than fifty relatives of Bach, whose names remain on record, were musicians.

Men have died from time to time, and worms have eaten them, but not for love.

Guy Davenport's account of a lunch with Thomas Merton—at which Merton devoured six martinis.

Spinach, fruit, water.

Having been Mahler's unvarying diet.

Ethiopians have black sperm, believed Herodotus.

A sort of gutless Kipling.

Orwell called Auden.

Ernest Poole. Margaret Wilson. Julia M. Peterkin. Margaret Ayer Barnes. T.S. Stribling.

Being five of the first fifteen winners of the Pulitzer Prize for fiction.

Caroline Miller. Josephine W. Johnson. Harold L. Davis.

Being the next three.

Ted Hughes's father was one of only seventeen survivors from an entire *regiment* annihilated at Gallipoli.

No death in my lifetime has hurt poets more.

Said Seamus Heaney at the 1998 funeral of Hughes himself.

I nauseate walking; 'tis a country diversion, I loathe the country.

Says someone in Congreve's *The Way of the World.*

I'm going. I find the company very uncongenital.

Says someone in a Gypsy Rose Lee mystery.

He had abroun hayre. His complexion exceeding faire—he was so faire they called him *the Lady of Christ's College.*

Being Milton, as reported by John Aubrey.

Paavo Nurmi died partially paralyzed.

Paavo Nurmi.

The French government provides the Paris Opera a subsidy of roughly $135,000,000 each year.

The United States gives the Metropolitan Opera less than $1,000,000.

At eighteen, John Stuart Mill spent several nights in jail for having distributed birth control pamphlets in a London slum.

Delmore Schwartz, in his disturbed final years, hearing voices—and insisting that they were directed at him from the spire of the Empire State Building.

The Book of Margery Kempe, evidently the first autobiography in English by a woman.

Surely the first to have been dictated—by an illiterate author.

Martin Heidegger's affair with Hannah Arendt—conducted in the main at a squalid hotel next to the Marburg railroad station.

Sainte-Beuve's affair with Victor Hugo's wife.

Teilhard de Chardin was forbidden by the Jesuits to publish any of his philosophical writings while he lived.

November 30, 1935, Fernando Pessoa died on.

Leuprolide acetate. Metoprolol. Hydrochlorothiazide. Atorvastatin. Aspirin. Salmeterol xinafoate. Flunisolide. Omeprazole. Loperamide hydrochloride. Simethicone. Calcium carbonate.

Or is Novelist forgetting one or two.

It is really most unfortunate that she rules out copulation.

Said Lytton Strachey of Virginia Woolf's major novels.

Jeanne Eagels. As the original Sadie Thompson.

Irene Papas, as Antigone.

Irene Papas, as Helen.

Stainless maiden amid the stain of blood.

Lucretius calls Iphigenia.

You never hear of a novel-wright or a picture-wright or a poem-wright—why a playwright?

Asked W.S. Gilbert.

When the stove is clean enough I shall turn on the gas.

Wrote Anna Wickham—twelve years before she hanged herself instead.

Where the synecdoche of *tessera* made a totality, however illusive, the metonymy of *kenosis* breaks this up into discontinuous fragments.

Somewhere declareth Harold Bloom.

It may be essential to Harold Bloom that his audience not know quite what he is talking about.

Commenteth Alfred Kazin—pointing out other immortal phrasings altogether.

How many of you are there in the quartet?

The affecting ancient legend that when Pindar was a youngster, bees once coated his lips with honey while he slept.

Alprazolam.

Robert Pershing Doerr.

Pausing to remember that no fewer than eight characters in *Hamlet*—eight—die violently.

The Theatre Sarah Bernhardt in Paris.

Whose name the Nazis changed during the occupation because of her having been a Jew.

174517—

Which Primo Levi could read tattooed on his left forearm from Auschwitz onward.

Light from the lighthouse at Alexandria, one of antiquity's Seven Wonders, was visible from as far as twenty miles at sea.

Helmut Newton died in a car crash. At eighty-three.

Trying to conceive of having attended Georgia State College for Women in the mid-1940s.

And wondering who in heaven's name there was for Flannery O'Connor to have a conversation with.

Paul Valéry's wife was a niece of Berthe Morisot—and had in fact posed for Morisot any number of times.

Alexander Blok's wife was the daughter of the chemist Mendeleyev.

Morningless sleep.

Epicurus called death.

Leonardo. Michelangelo. Botticelli. Raphael. Watteau. Claude. Van Dyck. Guido Reni. Pontormo. Poussin. Donatello. Reynolds.

Being but a handful among artists who never married.

An unpurchasable mind.

Shelley credited himself with.

Baudelaire, twice—in print—called upon Poe as a kind of patron saint to intercede for him during a prayer.

Malcolm Lowry, seemingly serious himself, told a friend he had once prayed to Kafka:

And he answered my prayer.

In addition to French, Delacroix read fluently in Greek, Latin, Italian, English, and evidently German.

Latin, French, Italian, and Flemish.

Rubens wrote letters in.

Jemand musste Josef K. verleumdet haben.

Pigalle's sculpture of a naked eighty-plus-year-old Voltaire—for which the body was posed for by a different elderly man altogether.

Saul Kripke had mastered advanced calculus before finishing grammar school.

In Omaha.

She Who Was Once the Helmet-Maker's Beautiful Wife.

Readers who assume that the title *Samson Agonistes* means something about Samson in pain.

After the breakthrough by Marian Anderson and Mattiwilda Dobbs, the next two dominant black singers at the Metropolitan were Leontyne Price and Martina Arroyo. Arroyo was frequently mistaken for Price. I'm the other one, love, she told the Met doorkeeper who got it wrong one morning.

Eyeless in Gaza, at the mill with slaves.

Fanny Burney's account of her surgery for breast cancer at fifty-nine, in 1811.

Before anesthesia.

Dwight Eisenhower was once asked by an assistant if he would like to meet Robert Frost, who happened to be visiting someone else at the White House.

Eisenhower could not think of a reason why he should bother.

A hetaera named Cyrene, remembered for 2,400 years—because Aristophanes indicates that she could perform in a dozen different positions.

Theoris and Archippe, two others remembered for slightly longer.

Because Sophocles had affairs with each.

Apelles' long-lost *Birth of Venus,* painted 1,800 years before Botticelli's—and said to have been a likeness of Phryne, the most beautiful of them all.

And all of whom must surely have been included in an equally irretrievable work by Suetonius—

His lost book entitled *On Famous Courtesans.*

Shakespeare's younger sister.

The Westminster Review called Emily Brontë.

Cervantes was a relative of his.

Kipling said of Mark Twain.

I think what attracted me was less art itself than the artist's life, the freedom to live as one pleased.

Said Bonnard, *re* having become a painter.

Nulla dies sine linea.

Not a day without a line, Pliny says Apelles said.

Oliver Wendell Holmes, Jr., was wounded three times in the Civil War.

John Simon's verdict that there were two things he was able to say about the poems of Robert Creeley:

They are short; they are not short enough.

It was I killed the old pawnbroker woman and her sister Lizaveta with an axe and robbed them.

March 13, 1979, Madeleine Grey died on.

Contemporary art criticism, second decade, fourteenth century. From the *Purgatorio:*

In painting Cimabue was thought to hold the field, but now Giotto has the cry, so that the other's fame grows dim.

Our sodomite-saint.

Malcolm Muggeridge called T.E. Lawrence.

Jack Daniel's Tennessee sour mash whiskey.

Being the best thing he knew about America, Jacques Lacan said.

A London street called Ropemaker's Lane, Daniel Defoe died in.

Gibbon, on Samuel Johnson:

Bigoted.

Boswell, on Gibbon:

Ugly, affected, disgusting.

It's a terrible thing to die young. Still, it saves a lot of time.

Quoth Grace Paley.

Bertrand Russell was born ten years before James Joyce, and died on Joyce's birthday—twenty-nine years after him.

Jane Avril died in an old people's home. Forty-one years after the death of Toulouse-Lautrec.

Nietzsche, who proclaimed that God was dead—but whose own coffin was adorned with a silvered cross.

Damn, I'm almost sorry you called. Can you even begin to guess how many friends of mine that makes, just in the past year or so?

I assume you're aware of something else too, chum? At our age, we don't replace them.

The failure of the 1853 premiere of Verdi's *La Traviatta*—essentially because the soprano was viewed as too plump for a heroine dying of tuberculosis.

Troppo prosperosa, being the Italian.

I think *A Bend in the River* is much, much better than Conrad.

Pronounced the humility-drenched author of *A Bend in the River.*

The acute suggestiveness in Pascal's apology for having written a particularly long letter.

Because he hadn't had the time to write a short one.

   Peoples bore me,
   literature bores me, especially great literature.

Says Henry in *The Dream Songs.*

The Homer of painting, Reynolds called Michelangelo.

The Homer of painting, Delacroix called Rubens.

Well, God has arrived. I met him on the 5:15 train.

Said Maynard Keynes, at a 1929 return of Wittgenstein to Cambridge after fifteen years away.

An eclectic realist of disputed merit.

The actual *catalogue* of the Metropolitan Museum once called Manet.

Miles Davis's speedometer had already reached 105 miles per hour, on New York's West Side Highway, when one of the people with him asked if he should be driving so fast.

I'm in here too, Davis's concept of reassurance was.

Corbière was dead at thirty.

Giorgione, at thirty-three or thirty-four.

Books weaken the memory.

Says Plato in the *Phaedrus.*

Machines cannot think.

Charles Ives gave away the cash that came with his Pulitzer Prize.

Badges of mediocrity, dismissing such awards as.

Created only for imbeciles, rogues, and rascals, Cézanne had had it.

Conversely Edvard Grieg, who displayed his medals unabashedly—particularly since they sped him through customs with all complications waived, he discovered.

The meaningless oddity that one of Washington's pet hounds at Mount Vernon—was named Truman.

The report that Turner, told he was dying, asked his doctor to leave the room for a glass of sherry and then to judge things again.

Which the doctor allegedly did—but with no change of diagnosis.

Amiri Baraka's slapdash, banal, repetitious, self-contradictory, mendacious poem, *Somebody Blew Up America.*

Novelist is forgetting odious.

He who writes for fools will always find a large audience.

Said Schopenhauer.

Tertian malaria, Velazquez died of.

The words *honest*—or *honesty*—occur fifty-two times in *Othello.*

Diodorus Siculus. Twelve volumes in the Loeb Classical Library.

Dio Cassius. Nine volumes.

Freud's first publication in English—via the Hogarth Press.

Which is to say, by Leonard and Virginia Woolf.

There's rosemary for you and rue for you.

Echoed John Webster—at most six years after Ophelia's earlier usage.

Ted Williams, bedded after a stroke, seen reaching out to lightly bat away a child's balloon—and missing.

Ted Williams.

Artists are the monks of the bourgeois state.

Said Cesare Pavese.

Les bourgeois, ce sont les autres.

Said Jules Renard.

Baudelaire wore rouge.

Because of global warming, the last snows will be gone from Kilimanjaro very possibly within Novelist's own remaining lifetime.

January 5, 1942, Tina Modotti died on.

Cardinal Newman, being directed by Everett Millais to a tall chair atop a platform where he was to sit for his portrait:

Your Eminence, on that eminence, if you please.

Abject bottom-licking narcissism—

Martha Gellhorn found in Hemingway.

Bogus, Zelda Fitzgerald's word for him was.

Dante Gabriel Rossetti's addiction to chloral hydrate. And whiskey.

There will always be another poet.

Said Stevie Smith.

You never paint the Parthenon; you never paint a Louis XV armchair. You make pictures out of some little house in the Midi, a packet of tobacco, or an old chair.

Said Picasso.

Until the election of Marguerite Yourcenar, in 1981, no woman had ever been named to the French Academy.

On the original title pages of Jane Austen, before the posthumous disclosure of her identity:

By a Lady.

Ray Bradbury's father was a telephone lineman.

His third wife, Lady Jean Campbell, in regard to life with Norman Mailer:

All we ever did was go to dinner with his mother.

No one has explained what the leopard was seeking at that altitude.

Constable. Etty. Haydon. Landseer. Leslie.

All of whom were pupils of Fuseli.

Pavel Tchelitchew. Wyndham Lewis. Roger Fry.

All of whom painted portraits of Edith Sitwell.

Jean Harlow was dead at twenty-six.

Old enough so that gradual loss of bone has left him at least two and a half inches shorter than he was when younger.

Life is a long process of getting tired.

Say Samuel Butler's *Notebooks.*

This is the foul fiend, Fibbertigibbet.

The first Crusade fought its way into Jerusalem in July of 1099. Some seventy thousand surviving Muslims—the majority being women and children—were methodically slaughtered. Such Jews as remained were burned alive in a synagogue.

All this being God's will, the Crusaders' motto reassured them.

George Sand did virtually all of her writing between midnight and six AM—and then slept until three in the afternoon.

Four years before Haydn's death in Vienna, somehow a rumor announcing same reached Paris—where Cherubini and Kreutzer composed music for a memorial.

What sport, if I had been able to appear and conduct the Mass myself, Haydn's reaction was.

Andrew Jackson was twelve years old when he enlisted to fight in the Revolutionary War.

I will not believe that a woman can draw so well.

Said Degas at his first view of a Mary Cassatt.

Andreas Baader. Gudrun Ensslin. Ulrike Meinhof.

Julius and Ethel Rosenberg were Brooklyn Dodgers fans.

Oscar Wilde's lecture tour of the United States—which brought him to St. Joseph, Missouri, only one week after the shooting of Jesse James.

    That dirty little coward
    Who shot Mister Howard
    And laid poor Jesse in his grave.

Irving Berlin had no schooling after the fifth grade.

Thomas Edison had only three months of actual classroom time.

Agatha Christie had none whatsoever.

One would like to curse them so that thunder and lightning strike them, hell-fire burn them, the plague, syphilis, epilepsy, scurvy, leprosy, carbuncles, and all diseases attack them. Ignorant asses.

Being Luther, in a contemplative mood *re* the papal hierarchy.

Frida Kahlo's amputated leg.

Mikhail Bakhtin's.

The last words of Mr. Despondency were, Farewell night; welcome day! His daughter went through the river singing, but no one could understand what she said.

Dr. Donne's verses are like the peace of God; they pass all understanding.

Said James I.

Among those mailing an order to Shakespeare and Company, in Paris, for an earliest copy of *Ulysses*—Winston Churchill.

July 17, 1974, Dizzy Dean died on.

Emerald eyes, Dante says Beatrice had.

While never telling us the color of her hair.

A writer of something occasionally like English—and a man of something occasionally like genius.

Swinburne called Whitman.

A man standing up to his neck in a cesspool—and adding to its contents.

Carlyle called Swinburne.

Jane Welsh Carlyle died a virgin.

The avant-garde. A kind of research and development arm of the culture industry, the critic Thomas Crowe called it.

It is utterly impossible to persuade an editor that he is nobody.

Said William Hazlitt.

Galen's astonishingly voluminous medical knowledge—much of it acquired while working as the surgeon at a gladiatorial school.

Pontormo's diary. Which generally concentrates more on the state of his bowels than on anything of interest in art history.

Among the worst books ever committed to paper.

An Archbishop of Canterbury called *Tess of the d'Urbervilles.*

A child's introduction to Nietzsche and Jung.

The Yale Review categorized Hesse's novels as.

The year lost to tuberculosis early in her career by Elisabeth Schwarzkopf—probably contracted in dank World War II Vienna air-raid shelters.

Mallarmé, never well-off, who nonetheless possessed works by Whistler, Monet, Berthe Morisot, Gauguin, Odilon Redon, and Rodin—all personal gifts.

Of contemporary literature, philosophy, and politics he appeared to know next to nothing.

We are told by Dr. Watson about Holmes.

Karl Marx died sitting at his desk.

Antonin Artaud, sitting up at the foot of his bed.

People who actually believe that Christo's tangerine-colored bedsheets fluttering about in New York's Central Park had something even remotely to do with art.

Oranges and lemons,
Say the bells of St. Clement's.

Alexander Fleming discovered penicillin only because a bacteria culture with which he was experimenting became contaminated—by accident.

Chesterfield's definition of the word *illiterate,* as a noun, 1748:

A man who is ignorant of Greek and Latin.

Matthew Arnold's of *philistine,* ca. 1869:

A person who believes his greatness is proved by being rich.

Barbarous, Samuel Pepys called *Hamlet.*

Jessica Lange was once a waitress in the Lion's Head.

Eve Ensler was once a waitress in the Lion's Head.

And yet it was impossible for me to say to men speak louder, shout, for I am deaf.

Mark Twain's pronouncement that the personages in a novel should be alive, except in the instance of corpses—and that the reader should be able to tell the corpses from the others.

Unfortunately not the case in Fenimore Cooper, he determines.

When I was boy, the Sioux owned the world; the sun rose and set on their land.

Said Sitting Bull.

When I was young I walked all over this country, east and west, and saw no other people than the Apaches.

Said Cochise.

Once I moved about like the wind. Now I surrender to you and that is all.

Said Geronimo.

Noting that the first word of English that Robinson Crusoe teaches his man Friday—after the name Friday itself—is *Master.*

Nathanael West once applied for a Guggenheim fellowship with recommendations from Scott Fitzgerald, Edmund Wilson, and Malcolm Cowley.

Guess.

Novelist's own Guggenheim applications, plural, with references equally as impressive.

Guess—six or seven times.

Comedy aims at representing men as worse, tragedy as better, than in actual life.

Says Aristotle.

Marco Polo died three years after Dante.

Horace Greeley died insane.

Future generations will regard Bob Dylan with the awe reserved for Blake, Whitman, Picasso and the like.

Said an otherwise seemingly rational writer named Jonathan Lethem.

D.H. Lawrence and Susan His Cow.

The 1940s network radio broadcast of *La Bohème* in which Toscanini could be distinctly heard humming along with Licia Albanese and Jan Peerce as he conducted.

Karl Popper claimed he had written the 480-plus pages of *The Open Society and Its Enemies* more than thirty times.

We did not ask you white men to come here.

Said Crazy Horse.

A heart attack while swimming, Theodore Roethke died of.

The greatest purveyor of violence in the world today, my own government, said Martin Luther King.

In 1967.

Georges Rouault was born during a bombardment in the Franco-Prussian War—in a Paris cellar.

Bob Dylan, as poet:

Sophomoric and obvious, said Ned Rorem.

Bob Dylan, as composer:

Banal and unmemorable, Rorem *aussi.*

April 21, 1924, Eleonora Duse died on.

For no reason whatsoever, Novelist has just flung his cat out one of his four-flights-up front windows.

Saint-Exupéry wrote *Le Petit Prince* while living on Long Island.

Well past fifty, Tolstoy began an intensive study of Hebrew with a Moscow rabbi—not very many years after having devoted similar concentration to mastering Greek.

The awareness of not having accomplished anything, and not expecting to accomplish anything in the future, is not so terrible because Tolstoy makes up for all of us.

Concluded Chekhov.

When will you pay me?
Say the bells of Old Bailey.

You go wherever you like. I'm not about to get myself killed for that wife Helen of yours.

Says Agamemnon to Menelaus—essentially about commencing the Trojan War—in the little that remains of a lost play by Euripides.

Act. *Then* call upon the gods.

Says another Euripides fragment.

That tampon painter.

Joan Mitchel called Helen Frankenthaler.

The friendship of Zola and Cézanne.

Tracing back to when they were boys of twelve and thirteen.

The big tragedy for the poet is poverty.

Said Patrick Kavanagh.

Try to get a living by the Truth—and go to the Soup Societies.

Lamented Melville rather earlier.

Qu'ils mangent de la brioche.

Top-heavy was the ship as a dinnerless student with all Aristotle in his head.

For a time, at the Tuileries, Napoleon kept the *Mona Lisa* in his bedroom.

Only this tardily realizing—that if he had not made use of his middle name, among the better-known twentieth-century American poets would be a William Williams.

One of the two listed witnesses at the wedding of Jackson Pollock and Lee Krasner, on lower Fifth Avenue in Manhattan, was the church janitor.

Turgenev was sentenced to a month in jail, and subsequent banishment from St. Petersburg, for the simple act of having written an obituary of Gogol, whose work was considered subversive by czarist authorities.

I absolutely cannot do without it.

Says Tchaikovsky's diary, about alcohol.

Veronese's *Finding of Moses,* at the Prado.

In which Pharaoh's daughter and her handmaidens are shown in clothing not worn until the Renaissance.

The last time anyone mentioned Erskine Caldwell.

Lorca was thirty-eight when he was murdered.

Everywhere Lorca went he found a piano.

Rafael Alberti remembered of him.

Met him pike hoses.

Had Sir Thomas Beecham ever conducted any Stockhausen?

No. But he believed he had trodden in some.

Before the Euro, the portrait of Yeats on Ireland's twenty-pound note.

America's Whitman twenty-dollar bill, when?

The Melville ten?

One of the rare pieces of expository writing by a woman in antiquity—a list of rules for behavior when visiting an exclusive house of prostitution.

Left by one Gnathaena, in third-century Athens, and actually catalogued in the great library of Alexandria until its destruction.

No more than ten or twelve weeks after an actress he had been living with took her own life, Gottfried Benn was engaged to another woman.

1427–1429. Being the closest one can evidently come to a date for the death of Masaccio.

The Threepenny Opera. For which Brecht stole much of the language from someone else's German translation of the original John Gay version—and for which he was ultimately forced to surrender part of his royalties.

Truth lies at the bottom of a well.

Cicero says Democritus said.

Truth lies at the bottom of a well.

Rabelais says Heraclitus said.

I've had it with those cheap sons of bitches who claim they love poetry but never buy a book.

Growled Kenneth Rexroth.

Novelist does not own a cat, and thus most certainly could not have thrown one out a window.

Nonetheless he would lay odds that more than one hopscotching reviewer will be reading carelessly enough here to never notice these two sentences and announce that he did so.

God help us, did I not tell your Grace that those were nothing but windmills?

All cats are grey in the dark.

What would *non-creative* writing be?

George Steiner once casually wondered.

Musicke, the Elizabethan spelling was.

Hydeous. Swolne. Perswasion. Sinne. Subtill.

Brightnesse falls from the ayre.

He would not blow his nose without moralising on the state of the handkerchief industry.

Said Cyril Connolly of Orwell.

Billy Graham's anti-Semitic exchange with Richard Nixon, as preserved on White House tapes.

E.M. Forster lived with his mother until her death when he was sixty-six.

Children of Palestrina, Verdi referred to Italian composers as.

Bastien-Lepage was dead at thirty-six.

Aubrey Beardsley was dead at twenty-five.

The somewhat notorious soprano Susanna Cibber. Who sang so movingly in an early performance of Handel's *Messiah* that a Dublin bishop informed her afterward that any and all of her earthly sins were therewith irrevocably forgiven.

Charlotte Brontë died in March of 1855.

The Reverend Arthur Nicholls, whom she had married nine months before, would live until 1906.

A daughter of Dickens lived until 1929.

After Jean Stafford, vacationing, had explained to a weathered Wyoming ranch hand how she made her living:

That's real nice work. I reckon you can even always arrange to do it in the shade.

Wondering why it always seems somehow not quite accurate—that Mozart was born only fourteen years before Beethoven.

Now I'll have *eine kleine* pause.

Said Kathleen Ferrier—dying.

British cavalry in the Crimean War were so scandalously ill-supplied and neglected that many starved to death—as did the very horses that had survived the Charge of the Light Brigade.

February 2, 1940, Meyerhold was executed on.

Picasso, *avec* laughter, after being asked if he had used models for *Les Demoiselles d'Avignon:*

Where would I have found them?

A dreadful old fraud.

Edmund Wilson called Robert Frost.

A sententious, holding-forth old bore who expected every hero-worshipping adenoidal little twerp of a student-poet to hang on his every word.

James Dickey would elaborate subsequently.

Edith Piaf was four feet eight inches tall.

George Lyman Kittredge, who taught Shakespeare at Harvard for forty-eight years—and demanded that all of his students memorize at least six hundred lines per semester.

Six hundred lines. The student reciting the entire *To be or not to be* soliloquy has mastered all of thirty-five.

Alexander the Great once watched in puzzlement as Diogenes sifted through a heap of human bones.

How strange, Diogenes finally decided—that I cannot make a distinction between those of your father and those of his slaves.

Ephesus, Mary Magdalen died in.

Ephesus, the Virgin Mary may have died in.

José Clemente Orozco lost his left hand in a college chemistry explosion.

Mr. McChoakumchild, Dickens names the demanding schoolmaster in *Hard Times.*

Almost an insult to the serious reader, Shaw said.

An abridged, accelerated, night-school course.

Eugenio Montale saw in Pound's version of culture in the *Cantos.*

Oh, Aaron Burr, what hast thou done?
Thou hast shooted dead that great Hamilton.

For a millennium, or longer, Greek and then Roman seamen along the coast of the Troad repeatedly *insisted* they had seen the ghosts of Achilles and/or Hector in full armor at the shore.

After Vicente Aleixandre's Nobel Prize, Madrid renamed the street on which he lived in his honor.

Which was to say that one could then write to Sr. Vicente Aleixandre—on Calle Vicente Aleixandre.

There's nothing more embarrassing than being a poet.

Suspected Elizabeth Bishop.

A remedy once suggested by Camille Pissarro for the betterment of French art:

Burn down the Louvre.

What I have always liked about this place are the windows.

Determined Bonnard, strolling through the same museum.

Mornings, when the leaves are dewy, some of them are like jewels where the earliest sunlight glistens.

A quirky new impulse of Novelist's, at news of several recent deaths—

Dialing the deceased, in the likelihood that no one would have yet disconnected their answering machines—and contemplating their voices one eerie final time.

A trampish sort of appearance.

Iris Murdoch recalled *re* Wittgenstein.

Joyce himself is an insignificant man, wearing very thick eyeglasses, dull, self-centered.

Says Virginia Woolf's diary.

Reality is under no obligation to be interesting.

Said Borges.

December 31, 1936, Unamuno died on.

October 18, 1955, Ortega.

Franklin D. Roosevelt, well into his political career, at least once wrote a book review.

Bach was fifteen when he began his professional music career.

As a boy soprano.

A quart or more of alcohol per day, uncounted amphetamines, uncounted aspirin, uncounted barbiturates—and at a minimum two packs of cigarettes.

Being Sartre in his most productive years.

The novels of Paul de Kock, which are admired by Molly Bloom.

As they were in fact by Karl Marx.

Dear President George W. Bush:

Herewith please find uncorrected proofs for the newly discovered rewritten version of Heidegger's *Sein und Zeit.* Kindly limit your review to twelve thousand words. Thank you.

John Kenneth Galbraith was made to repeat his senior year in high school.

Scarcely intelligible, Dryden labeled Shakespeare's language.

Quote: His whole style is so pestered with figurative expressions that it is as affected as it is coarse.

A jockey can earn more in one race than a schoolteacher is paid in an entire year.

Objected Juvenal—close to nineteen hundred years ago.

He who today writes artistically dies without recognition or reward.

Complained Lope de Vega—in 1609.

Landlords in lower Manhattan who were shrewd enough, over the years, to accept recent work by moneyless young artists instead of rent.

One of those, in the late 1940s, who wasn't—and rather than *two* paintings by Robert Rauschenberg insisted upon the month's $15.

Jaroslav Seifert, like Dostoievsky earlier, who once eluded execution only moments before the shots were to be fired.

Yet afterward insisted he was no more traumatized by the recollection than a youngster remembering last year's measles.

The nephew of Aeschylus named Philocles, also a playwright, all of whose plays are lost.

But who was talented enough to gain the prize for tragedy in the year when Sophocles presented *Oedipus Rex.*

A cask of brandy, Nelson's corpse was brought back to London in, after Trafalgar.

To slow decomposition.

Agonies of galloping speechlessness.

Beckett once talked of a writer's block as.

When you can see the bandwagon, it's already gone.

Said de Kooning.

Late-life Nietzsche postcards—that he signed *Kaiser Nietzsche.*

Freakish, Voltaire called the *Divine Comedy.*

Extravagant, absurd, disgusting.

Horace Walpole made it.

According to Ford Madox Ford, Flaubert once opened his front door to Henry James and Ivan Turgenev *in his dressing gown*—and thus offended James's sensibilities virtually beyond redemption.

The nicest old lady I ever met.

Faulkner decided to christen James.

Multiple surgical chain staples are evident in the right lung, consistent with prior resections.

Reads a recurrent notation in reports on Novelist's chest x-rays.

A post-Mao version of the Long March—which implies that forcibly conscripted porters carried him on a litter for much of the 5,000 miles.

All the ills from which America suffers can be traced back to the teaching of evolution.

Said William Jennings Bryan—in 1924.

Abortionists, feminists, gays, lesbians—all in good part responsible for 9/11, said Jerry Falwell.

I totally concur. Said Pat Robertson.

David Gascoyne's addiction to Benzedrene. And lighter-fluid fumes.

Look, look, master, here comes two religious caterpillars.

Remembering that Charles Darwin is buried in Westminster Abbey.

Fundamentalismbecility.

Django Reinhardt died of a cerebral hemorrhage—while fishing in the Seine.

People who actually believe that Damien Hirst's fourteen-foot shark in a tank of formaldehyde has something even remotely to do with art.

Our father who art in heaven
Stay there.

Requested Jacques Prévert.

Tamara Geva. Vera Zorina. Maria Tallchief. Tanaquil Le Clercq.

All of whom married George Balanchine.

Offensive, ill-written, mechanical. All in all, detestable.

Sainte-Beuve called the novels of Stendhal.

I count only on being reprinted in 1900.

Said Stendhal himself, who died in 1842.

I shall hear in heaven.

Which Beethoven did or did not say, nearing death.

Do Not Leave Car Unattendant.

Jean Giono was twice imprisoned for collaboration with the Nazis in World War II.

Englishing Pindar is so exacting, concluded Abraham Cowley, that if one were to attempt it *literally* it would sound as if one certifiable lunatic had translated another.

Mussorgsky and Rimsky-Korsakov were for a time roommates.

The first use of the word *classic* in its long since traditional sense—by the Latin critic Aulus Gellius, ca. 180AD.

I am no Einstein.

Once said Einstein.

Pope Eliot.

Dylan Thomas called him.

Michelangelo's *David* stood on the open porch of the Palazzo Vecchio, where Michelangelo had asked that it be placed, from 1504 until 1873—when Florence moved it into the Academy and out of the weather.

And to where some cretin a hundred and twenty years later would take a hammer to its left foot.

Only a single, incomplete manuscript of the *Annals* of Tacitus remained extant after the Dark Ages.

August 21, 2005, Dahlia Ravikovitch died on.

Pacing along as if they had an appointment at the end of the world—

Reads an Isak Dinesen description of a herd of elephants.

The ménage à trois involving Paul and Gala Eluard and Max Ernst—

After which Gala became Gala Dalí.

Simone de Beauvoir's affair with Nelson Algren.

Which she later infuriated him by writing about.

A leper and a sodomite.

Emerson called Swinburne.

Like a vile scum on a pond.

Pound viewed G.K. Chesterton.

Landskip, painters long spoke of it as.

Dreiser, years in advance, telling H.L. Mencken that he has already prepared his dying words:

Shakespeare, I come.

Alan Turing was dead at forty-one.

You don't have a computer? So how do you write your books? You don't still use a typing machine?

Wondering if anyone, ever, has listened to Elgar's first *Pomp and Circumstance* march without repeated irrepressible grins of delight?

I fear that I have just seen the greatest actor in the world.

Said Sarah Bernhardt of Nijinsky.

He eats with his knife and accompanies every gesture, every movement of his hand, with that implement, which he grasps firmly when he commences his meal and never puts down until he leaves the table.

Said Mary Cassatt *re* Cézanne—and what she also described as his total disregard for the dictionary of manners, unquote.

The likelihood that Lenin died of syphilis.

Raymond Chandler did not publish his first novel until he was fifty.

Dashiell Hammett published his fifth novel at thirty-nine—and not one thing else in the remaining twenty-seven years of his life.

Great Empedocles, that ardent soul,
Leapt into Etna, and was roasted whole.

Oh, that flagon, that wicked flagon! thought Rip—what excuse shall I make to Dame Van Winkle?
Chekhov's grandfather had been a serf.
The speculation that Horace's father, himself a manumitted slave, might also have been a Jew.
December 11, 1513, Pintoricchio died on.
So excessively did Shaw admire Strindberg that he actually used the money from his Nobel Prize to arrange for better English translations of Strindberg's plays.
John Steinbeck, asked if he felt he had in fact deserved his own Nobel Prize:
Frankly, no.
Thomas Nashe was dead at thirty-one. Where, of what, or even exactly when, remains unknown.
Zapata was thirty-nine when he was murdered.
Stephen Dedalus, at Sandymount, in 1904.
Is he aware that Yeats was born there?
Trollope's declaration that he wrote with his watch on the desk in front of him—so that he could be certain he had produced at least two hundred and fifty words every quarter of an hour.

The measure of a man's greatness would be in terms of what his work *cost* him.

Wittgenstein once told someone.

Picasso's admiration for Charlie Chaplin.

Diego Rivera's.

Stalin's.

As early as in Plutarch:

Let them who can do nothing better, teach.

Mr. Churchill, you are drunk.

And you, Madame, are ugly. But I shall be sober tomorrow.

The novels of Susan Sontag:

Self-indulgent overrated crap, the Kevin Costner character calls them in the movie *Bull Durham.*

From a letter of Balzac's, in his mid-thirties, recording that in a fit of creative frenzy he had just spent twenty-six consecutive days without once leaving his study:

Sometimes it seems to me that my very brain is on fire.

No further martinis after dinner, Conrad Aiken's physician once commanded.

Following which Aiken frequently refused to eat until practically bedtime.

If they do see fields blue, they are deranged, and should go to an asylum. If they only pretend to see them blue, they are criminals, and should go to prison.

Being Hitler—*re* artists he categorized as degenerate.

I shall fight as long as I live. And I shall not consider it more important to be alive than to be free.

Rang the first words of an oath taken by Athenians before battle.

The eighteenth-century evangelist George Whitefield. Whose pulpit voice was so effective, said David Garrick, that he could make listeners laugh or cry by no more than pronouncing the word *Mesopotamia.*

Gertrude Stein's Model T style, Elizabeth Hardwick called it.

There is one rule that can render your hand so light that the brush will float, says Cennino Cennini's handbook for painters, ca. 1435:

Do not enjoy too much the company of women.

Every drop of sperm spilled is a masterpiece lost.

Said Piet Mondrian, five hundred years later.

A damsel with a dulcimer
In a vision once I saw.

Piero della Francesca's *Nativity.* In which Joseph has removed the saddle of an ass to use as a seat—while the ass itself brays in the background.

Erik Satie lived the entire later half of his life in extreme indigence.

Incredulity that Schubert's Eighth Symphony—the *Unfinished*—was not once performed until thirty-seven years after his death.

Toasted Susie is my ice cream.

Pythagoras's insistence that in one of his earlier incarnations he had fought in the Trojan War.

In fact that he had been Euphorbus, who in the *Iliad* wounds Patroclus and is in turn killed by Menelaus.

Borges' vision of Paradise:

A kind of library.

The long-hoped-for opportunity to meet Byron that Schopenhauer turned away from at the last moment—when the woman he was with evinced far too much enthusiasm of her own about it.

Epi oinopa ponton.

Walter Scott's novels generally cost him innumerable hours of hunting through reference books.

Which were forever heaped up precariously on the floor below his desk.

In addition to Italian, Leopardi possessed effortless mastery of Greek, Latin, French, Spanish, English, and Hebrew—by the age of sixteen.

October 21, 1969, Jack Kerouac died on.

Romain Rolland never learned which side won World War II.

Wondering how many lifetime scribes and/or manuscript copyists were put out of work in the decades immediately after Gutenberg?

Wondering why the plural of *still life* is *still lifes* and not *still lives?*

Sofa-size.

Simone Weil was dead at thirty-four.

You have reached Ned Klein. Please leave a message after the beep.

When I am eighty, my art may finally begin to cohere. By ninety, it may truly turn masterful.

Said Hokusai. At seventy-three.

Windy humbuggeries.

Mark Twain found in Scott.

A hack writer who would not have been considered fourth-rate in Europe.

Faulkner once called Twain in turn.

The 2005 Vienna exhibition featuring erotic paintings by Gustav Klimt and Egon Schiele—at which patrons arriving nude or in skimpy bathing suits were admitted free.

Colossal ennui. It seems to me that I could write something like it tomorrow by taking inspiration from the cat walking over the keyboard on my piano.

Said Prosper Mérimée of *Tannhäuser.*

It is impossible to finish any of his plays, they are pitiful.

Claimed Napoleon *re* Shakespeare.

A lot of twaddle.

Confirmed George III.

More than sixty percent of the people in the United States do not know what the capitalized word *Holocaust* in its common contemporary usage stands for.

Assuming that Saul Bellow was aware of the Moses Herzog mentioned in passing in *Ulysses?*

A desperate Stevie Smith addict.

Sylvia Plath called herself.

April 16, 1958, Rosalind Franklin died on.

Capital punishment is our society's recognition of the sanctity of human life.

Declared a Utah senator named Orrin Hatch—presumably a former honors student in Logic 101.

Clov: What is there to keep me here?

Hamm: The dialogue.

The Girl of the Golden West, Act III—in which the soprano arrives on stage on horseback.

Renata Tebaldi was petrified.

One of the earliest translations of the Bible in America—into Mohawk.

At one juncture during his years as a customs inspector on the New York docks, Melville was forced to take a cut in salary—from $4.00 to $3.60 per day.

Oscar Hammerstein's first job in America, in a cigar factory, paid him two dollars a week.

Andrew Carnegie's, in a cotton mill, had paid $1.50—for twelve-hour days.

Washington Square, in Greenwich Village, Edward Hopper died in.

Washington Square, in Greenwich Village, Novelist also happens to be typing this last book only short blocks away from.

Lorenzo de' Medici, who commissioned Botticelli's *Birth of Venus,* ca. 1485.

And a dozen or so years later sent Amerigo Vespucci sailing westward.

To cause justice to prevail in the land.

To prevent the strong from oppressing the weak.

To better the welfare of the people.

—Read portions of the Code of Hammurabi—from what may have been as early as 1800BC.

Anthony Burgess's bad eyesight.

Which permitted him to once enter a bank in Stratfordon-Avon—and order a drink.

Lloyd George knew my father,
Father knew Lloyd George.

In 1907, Caruso was being paid $2,000 per performance at the Metropolitan.

$2,000 in *1907* currency.

The uncanny sense of *atmosphere* in certain Constable landscapes.

So that looking at them could make one worry that he might need an umbrella, Fuseli said.

Remembering next to nothing about *The Courtship of Miles Standish*—except that Longfellow himself was in fact descended from Priscilla and John Alden.

Mozart wrote his Thirty-Sixth Symphony, the *Linz,* in at most three days.

In the period when artists of stature were called upon to paint likenesses of hunted murderers on the walls of Florentine buildings, Andrea del Castagno's led to so many captures that he became known as *Andrea degli Impiccati*—Andrea of the Hanged.

Bach almost persuades me to be a Christian.

Roger Fry said.

January 11, 1966, Giacometti died on.

The Marquis de Sade was at least once arrested for sodomy. And once for severely beating a young woman.

While also being implicated in the deaths of two prostitutes after an overdose of aphrodisiacs during an orgy.

Listen, I bought your latest book. But I quit after about six pages. That's all there is, those little things?

We evaluate artists by how much they are able to rid themselves of convention.

Said Richard Serra.

I skate to where the puck is going to be, not where it's been.

Said Wayne Gretzky.

Ivy Compton-Burnett died after a bronchitis attack.

Martin Luther King's seminary studies—during which he received a grade of C in public speaking.

A street in Nice is named after Marie Bashkirtseff.

Mr. James Joyce is a great man who is entirely without taste.

Said Rebecca West.

He started off writing very well, then you can see his going mad with vanity. He ends up a lunatic.

Added Evelyn Waugh.

Very dirty and completely worthless.

Edith Sitwell called *Lady Chatterley's Lover.*

Wholly ignorant.

Waugh called Sitwell.

Wonderful, this death.

Allegedly said William Etty, as it occurred.

Oliver Goldsmith was the oldest member of his graduating class at Trinity College, Dublin.

And the lowest ranked.

Proust, in the equivalent of basic training during his one year of military service at eighteen, was ranked seventy-third in a platoon of seventy-four.

An incomparable painting by Apelles, which Augustus brought from Cos to Rome, where it was slightly damaged.

And where not one contemporary Roman artist had the confidence to attempt to restore it.

Auden's notion that one could readily imagine a young Tolstoy or Stendhal or Dostoievsky in a bar fight.

But Henry James, never.

There is nothing new to be discovered in physics now.

Concluded Kelvin. In 1900.

I would go to considerable expense and inconvenience to avoid his company.

Quoth John Cheever—*re* John Updike.

Euripides' father may have been a tavern-keeper.

Still curious all these years later as to why Faulkner would have given two of his major characters names then current in widely syndicated comic strips.

Though for that matter he gave three others the names of buildings on the University of Mississippi campus.

A passage in Montaigne where he speaks of himself as being well on the road to old age—having long since passed forty.

Mr. Salteena was an elderly man of forty-two.

Writes Daisy Ashford.

Anacreon, so highly acclaimed as a poet that the Athenians placed a statue of him on the Acropolis.

And so well known for other proclivities that Pausanias says the statue showed him drunk.

November 30, 1943, Etty Hillesum died on.

I become insane, with long intervals of horrible insanity. During these fits of absolute unconsciousness I drink, God only knows how often or how much.

Wrote Poe to a friend.

Reading a book in translation:

Like gazing at a Flemish tapestry with the wrong side turned out, said Cervantes.

Traduttore, traditore—translator, traitor, the Italian has it.

Pelham Grenville Wodehouse, his full name was.

Frank Raymond Leavis.

John Ronald Reuel Tolkien.

A century before Alcoholics Anonymous, something called the Sons of Temperance, Poe did make a stab at. To no avail.

Inscribed on a painting by Jacob Jordaens:

Nihil similius insano quam ebrius—Nothing is more similar to a lunatic than a drunkard.

According to Liszt, Chopin had blue eyes.

According to everyone else they were brown.

The man who eats in idleness what he has not earned is a thief.

Wrote Rousseau.

Catherine the Great died after having suffered a stroke and fallen from a commode in the royal water closet.

Eric Andrews here. Well, actually not here. But I'll get back to you as soon as I can. Please wait for the signal.

Giuseppe Ungaretti's father was a construction worker on the Suez Canal.

The Homeric combat between Norman Mailer and Gore Vidal at a 1977 cocktail party—

In which Mailer threw a drink into Vidal's face—and Vidal bit Mailer on the finger.

Chipping Sodbury General Hospital, near Bristol, J.K. Rowling was born at.

Rilke's over-sentimentalizing of the poor.

Did he ever once sit shivering in an attic? Kurt Tucholsky asked.

Why did Harper Lee never write another novel?

First, check the acoustics. Then make sure you know where the fire axe is.

Being Charles Mingus—offering advice *re* performing in unfamiliar basement jazz clubs.

Intellectual—hen-pecked you all.

Being Byron—reaching about as far as possible for a rhyme in *Don Juan.*

So exhaustive was Raphael's study of ancient sculpture in Rome that the city itself named him Keeper of Inscriptions and Remains.

Prokofiev was fifteen years older than Shostakovich.

The presumably apocryphal tale about a production of *Othello* by touring actors in the nineteenth-century American West—near the last lines of which a cowboy in the audience shot Iago dead on the spot.

Broken Arrow, Oklahoma, Warren Spahn died in.

Because of having lived openly with George Henry Lewes, who was married, George Eliot was denied burial in Westminster Abbey.

I have a truly marvelous demonstration of this proposition which this margin is too narrow to contain.

The last time anyone mentioned James Jones.

March 22, 1417, Nicolas Flamel died on.

In 1760, one year after Handel's death, a biography by a Reverend John Mainwaring.

Apparently the first ever written of a composer.

Like being increasingly penalized for a crime you haven't committed.

Says an Anthony Powell character about growing old.

Toscanini's seven-year affair with Geraldine Farrar—which he ended only when Farrar finally insisted that he leave his wife.

Ernest Hemingway's entire front-line service in Italy in World War I, before he was wounded by shell fragments, had added up to less than one week.

146

Handing out cigarettes and chocolate at a Red Cross canteen.

The greatest kindness we can show some of the authors of our youth is not to reread them.

Said François Mauriac.

Being reminded that Fermat was a magistrate—for whom mathematics was fundamentally a hobby.

I am half sick of shadows, said
The Lady of Shalott.

Tirra lirra, by the river
Sang Sir Lancelot.

Wondering if there is any viable way to convince critics never to use the word *tetralogy* without also adding that each volume can be readily read by it-self?

Alessandro Manzoni spent five years on the first two drafts of *I Promessi Sposi*—and twelve more on the final version.

Lulu slept naked because she liked to feel the sheets caressing her body and also because laundry was expensive.

Readily read?

A drawing by Rubens, in Rotterdam, of Achilles driving his spear into Hector's throat—with his left hand.

When Homer specifically describes him as using his right.

The Trojan War will not take place, Cassandra!
I will make you a bet on that, Andromache.
—Reads an exchange in *Tiger at the Gates.*
I just pretend.
Explained Laurence Olivier.
A pale, gentle, frightened little man.
Robert Louis Stevenson's wife described a not yet middle-aged Thomas Hardy as.

Berlioz read every Fenimore Cooper novel as quickly as it appeared.

And admitted that fully four hours after he finished *The Prairie* he was still weeping over the death of Natty Bumppo.

The classic orator Hyperides, who divided his time between homes in Athens, Piraeus, and Eleusis.

Depending upon which of his mistresses he felt like visiting.

Georges Simenon's affair with Josephine Baker.

Chardin died at eighty—without ever once in his life having ventured farther away from Paris than the forty miles to Fontainebleau.

Shakespeare never had six lines together without a fault. Perhaps you may find seven, but this does not refute my general assertion.

Johnson told Boswell.

Chingachgook—

Pronounced Chicago, I think, said Mark Twain.

Altogether impoverished in his early years in Paris, for a time Juan Gris did not even possess a bed—and slept on newspapers.

Kees van Dongen's admission that there were occasions during his own early Montmartre years when he was forced to filch milk and/or bread from neighborhood doorsteps—with an accomplice named Picasso.

Let there be Maecenases and there will be no lack of Virgils.

Said Martial.

Well, my own work, I am risking my life for it and my reason has half foundered because of it—that's all right.

Says a last unfinished letter of van Gogh's found after his death.

The poetry of the sane man vanishes into nothingness before that of inspired madness.

Said Socrates.

Gris was dead at forty. Of uremia.

August 28, 1947, Manolete died on.

Recalled from Eastern European ghettos, virtually until the very last residents were evacuated to Nazi death camps—schoolchildren reading Yiddish editions of *The Prince and the Pauper* and *Around the World in Eighty Days.*

God of forgiveness, do not forgive those murderers of Jewish children here.

Said Elie Wiesel, visiting at Auschwitz a half-century later.

Wait. Don't carry away that arm till I've taken off my ring.

Said Raglan during surgery after Waterloo.

Learning that there actually was an apple tree outside Newton's window at his mother's home.

Indeed an entire apple orchard.

Not a composer. A kleptomaniac.

Stravinsky called Benjamin Britten.

The appointment of a woman to public office is an innovation for which the public is not prepared, nor am I.

Determined Jefferson.

As many as five little-documented years passed between Shakespeare's departure from the Globe, at forty-seven or forty-eight, and his death in Stratford.

After thirty-seven plays, and probably parts of others, plus the poems—did he have no inclination to write *anything* in those last years?

Or does there appear a possibility that he sometimes collaborated with others and/or doctored their work anonymously?

Poetry makes nothing happen.

Auden said.

I will not go down to posterity speaking bad grammar.

Said Disraeli, correcting one of his final speeches.

Whether posterity will give us a thought I don't know. But we surely deserve one.

Wrote Pliny the Younger to Tacitus—in the early second century AD.

I'm a poet, I'm life. You're an editor, you're death.

Proclaimed Gregory Corso to someone in the White Horse Tavern—who shortly commenced punching him through the door and across the sidewalk.

Taking no more account of the wind that comes out of their mouths than that which they expel from their lower parts.

Leonardo described his response to critics as.

Ancora imparo, said Michelangelo at eighty-seven.

Still, I'm learning.

More true poetical genius as a painter than possessed by perhaps any other.

Joshua Reynolds saw in Julio Romano.

Me retracto de todo lo dicho, I take back everything I told you.

Announced Nicanor Parra at the end of each of his poetry readings.

Everything useful is ugly.

Said Gautier.

I never saw an ugly thing in my life.

Said Constable.

The rumor that Gainsborough deliberately painted his *Blue Boy* to mock Reynolds' academic insistence that blue was a color for use in backgrounds only.

Nicanor Parra's day job—

Professor of theoretical physics at the University of Chile.

Miroslav Holub's—

Chief research immunologist at the Czechoslovak Academy of Sciences.

Dr. Franz Kafka, the gravestone names him.

Apropos of his Doctor of Laws degree.

Superimposed metastatic disease would be difficult to exclude in this region.

Reads a gladsome evaluation in the analysis of Novelist's most recent bone scan.

So debilitatingly paranoid was Kurt Gödel in his later years, over imagined plots to poison him, that he essentially refused to eat.

And died weighing no more than sixty-five pounds.

Art cannot rescue anybody from anything.

Says the narrator of a Gilbert Sorrentino story.

The world has no pity on a man who can't do or produce something it thinks worth money.

Says Gissing in *New Grub Street.*

And to this day is every scholar poor:
Gross gold from them runs headlong to the boor.

Says Marlowe, in *Hero and Leander.*

October 8, 1963, Remedios Varo died on.

We have not seen a single Jew blow himself up in a German restaurant.

Pointed out the disaffected Muslim Wafa Sultan in 2006.

As Dickensian as anything Dickens ever wrote.

Graham Greene labeled W.C. Fields.

Maidservant gallantries, Constanza accused Mozart of.

Flaubert soils the brook in which he washes.

Said the critic Saint-Victor of *L'Éducation senti-mentale.*

M. Flaubert n'est pas un écrivain.

Said *Le Figaro* of *Madame Bovary.*

Why, this is very midsummer madness.

We live not as we will—but as we can.

Said Menander.

Cocteau, meeting Diaghilev for the first time, and asking what he might do to involve himself in ballet—

Astonish me, Diaghilev tells him.

Demodocus, the blind bard whose songs of the fall of Troy evoke tears in *Odyssey* VIII.

Could he have perhaps been the source of the legend that Homer himself was blind?

Languidezza per il caldo—Languidly, because of the heat.

Suggests Vivaldi's notation over the *Summer* segment of *The Four Seasons.*

For several hundred years, more than half a millennium after her death, coins bearing Sappho's likeness were minted on Lesbos.

In all the centuries since history began, we know of no woman who can truly be said to rival her as a poet.

Said Strabo, equally as long after her era.

Rheumatic fever, Robert Burns died of.

The report that to keep him from sitting with a book for sixteen hours a day, Edmund Wilson's parents bought him a baseball uniform. Which he happily put on—and sat in with a book for sixteen hours a day.

By way of an inheritance, Carl Jung's wife was one of the most wealthy women in Europe.

Anyone who would employ the word *diarrheic* to describe a book as exactingly crafted in every line as *Ulysses* has either never read eleven consecutive words or possesses the literary perception of a rutabaga.

Ulysses. Diarrheic, unquote. Dale Peck.

Somewhat similarly, Roddy Doyle. A complete waste of time—*Finnegans Wake.*

Though in his instance at least acknowledging that he had read only three pages.

America's Emily Dickinson dime?

Won't you come into the garden? I would like my roses to see you.

Once said Richard Brinsley Sheridan to a pretty girl.

My whole life is messed up with people falling in love with me.

Once said Edna St. Vincent Millay.

Even more incomprehensible than the two-century neglect of a painter like Vermeer—the *three* centuries in which the music of Monteverdi was all but forgotten.

January 10, 1957, Gabriela Mistral died on.

Tolstoy's ruined teeth.

Gogol's.

Admire a small ship, but put your cargo in a large one.

Hesiod said.

Savonarola, in one of his inflammatory sermons, directs his words at contemporary artists:

I tell you, the Virgin dressed herself as a poor woman. And you represent her as a whore.

This approximately one hundred years before he might have been able to view Caravaggio's version of her death—effected with such prototypal naturalism that her feet are not clean.

A critic. Someone who meddles with something that is none of his business.

Gauguin says Mallarmé said.

In flight from the Gestapo while a member of the French Resistance, Paul Eluard at one point hid for two months in an insane asylum.

Sartre's *The Respectful Prostitute* was first produced in Paris precisely in the middle of a campaign against immorality.

And had to be advertised with the word *Putain* blacked out.

Homer. Euripides. Ovid's *Metamorphoses.*

Being the works that Milton, blind, most frequently asked to have read to him.

Novalis's *Heinrich von Ofterdingen.*

The last one that Borges asked to hear before his death.

October 17, 1973, Ingeborg Bachmann died on.

Sit in thy cell—and thy cell shall teach thee all things.

Said Saint Anthony.

Who evidently sat in his own for as long as twenty years without once taking any sort of bath—or even washing his face.

Lauritz Melchior and Helen Traubel, for years two of the Metropolitan's central Wagnerians—who expended endless ingenuity in forever attempting to make each other break up into onstage laughter.

Trying to think of a single book by a significant writer as transparently spurious throughout as *A Moveable Feast.*

Wine, the title of John Gay's first published poem was.

In which he insisted that no one who drank only water could ever become an author.

One's first glass of the day is a great event.

Acknowledged Thackeray.

Not drunk is he who from the floor
Can rise alone and still drink more.

Contributed Thomas Love Peacock.

Bo-ray pri ha-gofen.

A manual-winding pocket watch, Einstein carried.

Snivel in a wet hanky, D.H. Lawrence called *Lord Jim.*

At fifty-eight, two years before his death, Chaucer was sued over a debt of fourteen pounds.

And did not have the money.

Gide-ists. Rilke-ists. Fraudulent existential witch doctors. Pallid worms in the cheese of capitalism. *Intellectuals.*

Being among Pablo Neruda's more kindly appellations for authors not concerned with politics.

Little more than a device for getting revenge upon those who are having a better time on earth.

Mencken called the Christian concept of immortality.

Was it Eliot's toilet I saw?

Inquired someone's palindrome—after use of a bathroom at Faber and Faber.

Well over a century after Dostoievsky's death in St. Petersburg, a great-grandson named Dmitri Dostoievsky still lived there—working as a tram driver.

Twenty-some years after Missolonghi, Teresa Guiccioli married a Parisian marquis—who was known to habitually introduce her as *Ma femme, ancienne maîtresse de Byron.*

August Comte married a prostitute.

Ibsen's terror of even the smallest dog.

The morning's recollection of the emptiness of the day before.

Its anticipation of the emptiness of the day to come.

Zurbarán died penniless.

The final entry *re* Frans Hals, dated September 1, 1666, in the records of the Haarlem Paupers' Fund—listing four florins for a gravedigger.

An immense nausea of billboards, Baudelaire spoke of.

A century and a half ago.

Closing time in the gardens of the West, Cyril Connolly called it.

A century after that.

What can be the sufficient reason for this phenomenon? said Pangloss.

It is the Last Day! cried Candide.

A man may know that he is going to die, but he can never know that he is dead.

Said Samuel Butler.

Death is not an event in life; we do not live to experience death.

Said Wittgenstein.

Versailles, Edith Wharton was buried in.

January 8, 1713, Arcangelo Corelli died on.

Blake's bust in Westminster Abbey.

By Jacob Epstein.

Epstein is a great sculptor. I wish he would wash. Said Pound.

The limpest of handshakes, Robert Graves said Pound had.

The mirror will not be looked into until you have returned.

Says a letter from the wife of an ancient Chinese poet.

Incapacitated by Alzheimer's disease, de Kooning was once discovered about to spike his coffee with weed killer—presumably thinking it whiskey.

Burton's *Anatomy of Melancholy*.

The only book that ever took him out of bed two hours sooner than he wished to be, Johnson said.

Chloroform in print.

Mark Twain called the Book of Mormon.

Think of the Bible and Homer, think of Shakespeare and think of me.

Unquote, Gertrude Stein.

Oh, dear—

Reportedly having been David Garrick's dying words.

Eddie Grant, the pre – World War I third baseman, who graduated from Harvard—and who insisted on shouting *I have it* instead of *I got it* when chasing a fly ball.

And who as an infantry captain would be killed by machine gun fire in the Argonne Forest.

Baseball is what we were, football is what we have become.

Said Mary McGrory.

Far too much music finishes far too long after the end.

Judged Stravinsky.

Still to be read in the blank spaces on some of Raphael's preliminary sketches for his Vatican *stanze* frescoes—drafts of love poems to his latest mistress.

Will Durant's amusingly unworldly conclusion that the Sappho in Raphael's *Parnassus* is—quote—too beautiful to be a lesbian.

Hark, Hark, the Lark! and *Who Is Sylvia?*

Which Schubert set on the same single afternoon.

The word *plagiarism*—from the Latin for kidnapping.

To kidnap another writer's brains, Martial had it.

Old Hoss. Old Pete. Old Reliable. Old Folks. Old Aches and Pains.

Novelist's personal genre. In which part of the experiment is to continue keeping him offstage to the greatest extent possible—while compelling the attentive reader to perhaps catch his breath when things achieve an ending nonetheless.

Conclusions are the weak point of most authors.

George Eliot said.

If you know what you're doing, you don't get intercepted.

Said Johnny Unitas.

Eugene Sue, most of whose widely read novels dealt with the poor and downtrodden.

And thereby made him a millionaire, Kierkegaard noted.

Picasso, in Paris during the Nazi occupation and learning that someone had accused him of having Jewish blood:

I wish I had.

Drawing, for an artist:

A way of thinking, Valéry termed it.

February 23, 1931, Nellie Melba died on.

Let me alone. Good day.

Said Tom Paine—to the two clergymen who had contrived to make their way to his bedside when he lay dying.

How long the days for the wretched, how swift for the favored.

Said Publilius Syrus.

'Tis their will—that thy son from this crested wall of Troy be dashed to death.

The most tragic of the poets.

Aristotle called Euripides.

Proust's excessively lavish over-tipping.

Gide's reputation as a cheapskate.

Coryate, the English traveler, in Venice in 1611:

When I went to the theatre, I observed certain things I never saw before; for I saw women acte.

Reminding one that Ophelia, Juliet, Rosalind, Cleopatra, Lady Macbeth—were all written to be portrayed by adolescent boys.

Until 1660, when one Margaret Hughes broke the English barrier as Desdemona.

Typhus, or his syphilis, caused Beethoven's deafness—question mark.

A rejection of all that civilization has done.

Said the *London Times* of a first Post-Impressionist exhibition, in 1910—which included Cézanne, van Gogh, Gauguin, Matisse, Picasso, others.

Just an old queen, Auden spoke of himself as.

While also referring to *Miss God.*

One never steps twice into the same Auden.

Randall Jarrell said.

Seneca's *Thyestes,* in which Thyestes unknowingly eats the flesh of his own children.

And is described as belching contentedly.

Twickenham, Alexander Pope was buried in.

Wondering how on earth one remembers—that when St. John of the Cross escaped after his near death by starvation in a Toledo prison, the first meal he was given, at a discalced Carmelite convent—was of pears simmered with cinnamon.

A good man—but he did not know how to paint.

Said El Greco of Michelangelo.

Oliver Wendell Holmes, Jr., at eighty-seven, seen turning to gaze after an attractive girl:

Oh, to be seventy again!

I must ever have some Dulcinea in my head—it harmonises the soul.

Said Laurence Sterne.

The pain of rereading *Twelfth Night* after far too many years and coming upon the end of the Clown's song in II.iii—

Then come kiss me, sweet-and-twenty,
Youth's a stuff will not endure.

Old age is not for sissies.

Said Bette Davis.

Tell me honestly, Cal. Am I as good a poet as Shelley?

Asked William Carlos Williams, not long before his death, of Robert Lowell.

Freud, born in 1856, being asked in 1936 how he felt:

How a man of eighty feels is not a topic for conversation.

Shaw, at ninety-four, being asked the same:

At my age, one is either well or dead.

Leukemia, Ernestine Schumann-Heink died of.

He was greater than we thought.

Said Degas at the funeral of Manet.

Apollinaire, who was severely wounded in World War I.

And then died of influenza two days before the Armistice.

December 8, 1918, Cpl. David Markson died on.

Human life is everywhere a state in which much is to be endured, and little to be enjoyed.

Declares a line in *Rasselas.*

The Rokeby Venus. Which was purchased in Yorkshire in the early 1800s for five hundred pounds.

And sold to the National Gallery in 1906 for ninety times that amount.

Samoa, Robert Louis Stevenson died in.

The Marquesas, Gauguin.

Tchaikovsky, Glinka, Borodin, Mussorgsky—all buried in the same St. Petersburg cemetery.

Diogenes, asking to be buried face downward—

Because the world will soon enough be turned upside down.

Every man is condemned to death—but with an indefinite reprieve.

Hugo said.

Those who know do not speak.

Those who speak do not know.

Forty-two, Kierkegaard died at.

There's nothing in the world for which a poet will give up writing, not even when he is a Jew and the language of his poems is German.

Said Paul Celan.

It would have been our pleasure to be bombed.

Said a survivor of Auschwitz.

August 8, 1596, Hamnet Shakespeare died on.

July 11, 1649, Susanna Shakespeare Hall died on.

February 7, 1662, Judith Shakespeare Quinney died on.

Virgil's ceaseless revisions of the *Aeneid.*

Writing only a few lines at a time and then licking them into shape as the she-bear does its cubs, Suetonius says he said.

One man is as good as another until he has written a book.

Said Benjamin Jowett.

To an astronomer, man is but an insignificant dot in an infinite universe—said whoever.

Though that insignificant dot is also the astronomer—said Einstein.

Please don't get up, I'm only passing through.

No more firing was heard at Brussels—the pursuit rolled miles away. Darkness came down on the field

164

and city; and Amelia was praying for George, who was lying on his face, dead, with a bullet through his heart.

What he had seen, was it a battle? And if so, was that battle Waterloo?

Thy labours shall outlive thee.

Wrote John Fletcher in lines dedicated to Ben Jonson.

Who spent his last years partially paralyzed and virtually alone—and in calamitous want.

Wondering when the last day may have passed—anywhere in the world—during which someone did not die in an act of religion-inspired terrorism.

Just glance around you: wars, catastrophes and disasters, hatreds and persecutions, death awaiting us at every side.

Commented Ionesco.

Acheron. Cocytus. Styx. Phlegethon. Pyriphlegethon. Lethe.

Late February or early March, 1945.

Anne Frank.

What see'st thou else.

In the dark backward and abysm of time?

His powers of mind have almost entirely left him; his late paintings are miserable; it is really a lamentable thing that a man should outlive his faculties.

Said Samuel Morse after a visit with an elderly John Singleton Copley.

You don't always *make* an out. Sometimes the pitcher *gets* you out.

Said Carl Yastrzemski.

In the long run we are all dead.

Noted Keynes.

When I went to America, my very first inquiry was concerning Melville. There was some slight evidence that he was alive, and I heard from Mr. E.C. Stedman, who seemed much astonished at my interest in the subject, that Melville was dwelling somewhere in New York.

Charidas, what is it like down there?

All darkness.

And resurrection?

All a lie.

—Quoth Callimachus.

Minor authors—who lived, men knew not how, and died obscure, men marked not when.

Roger Ascham takes notice of.

Those rare intellects who, not only without reward, but in miserable poverty, brought forth their works.

Vasari likewise commemorates.

One must go on working. And one must have patience.

Rodin told Rilke.

My time will come.

Said Gregor Mendel, ignored throughout his life.

On van Gogh's bier at Auvers-sur-Oise—clusters of golden sunflowers.

Brought by Dr. Gachet.

The report that Osip Mandelstam spent the last hours before his death in Siberia reading Petrarch—by firelight.

O lente lente currite noctis equi.

Verdi's funeral—which according to his own wishes was conducted without music.

Verdi's.

Though in fact he had asked that the score of his *Te Deum,* one of the *Four Sacred Pieces,* be placed in his coffin.

Regensburg, Johannes Kepler was buried in.

Where there, long unknown.

My old paintings no longer interest me. I'm much more curious about those I haven't done yet.

Said Picasso, at seventy-nine.

Kynge Arthur is nat dede but shall come agayne.

I'm cold, Snowden said. I'm cold.

For sundry doctrinal reasons, the Archbishop of Paris refused to sanction a Catholic burial for Colette.

Conversely, France itself granted her a state funeral—making her the first woman ever so honored.

Give me your arm, old toad;
Help me down Cemetery Road.

I have often thought of death, but now it is never out of mind.

Said Swift, in his late sixties—a decade before it actually occurred.

You can tell from my handwriting that I am in the twenty-fourth hour. Not a single thought is born in me that does not have death graven within.

Wrote Michelangelo at eighty-one—himself with eight years remaining.

The long littleness of life.

Frances Cornford speaks of.

As he reclined at table, there arose a question what sort of death was best. At which he immediately, before anyone could speak, said, A sudden one.

Says Dryden's Plutarch, *re* Caesar.

Philosophy ought really to be written only as a poetic composition.

Wittgenstein once suggested.

Merde pour la poésie.

Decided Rimbaud.

Timor mortis conturbat me.

Being William Dunbar—The fear of death distresses me.

And which Novelist is quite certain he has quoted before in his life.

Memento mori.

Any man if he is all alone becomes more aware of being lonely as he ages.

Said Eliot.

Nothing is more evident than that the decays of age must terminate in death; yet there is no man, says Tully, who does not believe that he may yet live another year.

Johnson is somewhere reminded.

The last act is tragic, however happy all the rest of the play.

Perceives Pascal.

Lorenzo da Ponte's memoirs—in which Mozart is practically never mentioned.

I've no more sight, no hand, nor pen, nor inkwell. I lack everything. All I still possess is will.

Said Goya—nearing eighty.

With an ink too thick, with foul pens, with bad sight, in gloomy weather, under a dim lamp, I have composed these pages. Do not scold me for it!

Appended Telemann to the score of some light soprano airs—written at eighty-one.

Time rushes by, love rushes by, life rushes by, but the red shoes dance on.

What happens in the end?

Oh, in the end she dies.

Twenty-five years after his death, Poe's remains were disinterred from what had been little better than a pauper's grave and reburied more formally.

Walt Whitman, who made the journey from Camden to Baltimore in spite of being disabled from a recent stroke, was the only literary figure to appear at the ceremonies.

O that it were possible
We might but hold some two days' conference
With the dead.
—Laments Webster's Duchess.

Celan's recollection that his mother had never had white hair.

Because of having been murdered in a concentration camp while still too young.

Cézanne, who lived in greater and greater isolation, late in life.

Degas, who lived in greater and greater isolation, late in life.

A hundred cares, a tithe of troubles, and is there one who understands me?

dein goldenes Haar Margarete
dein aschenes Haar Sulamith

In addition to his name and date on the frame of a portrait by Jan van Eyck:

Als ick kan—The best I can do.

Time hath, my lord, a wallet at his back,
Wherein he puts alms for oblivion.

Saint Gildas the Wise, of Wales, who asked that at his death he be placed in a small boat and set adrift at sea.

Sophocles, *re* a tremor in his hand, as recorded by Aristotle:

He said he could not help it; he would happily rather not be ninety years old.

It is later than you know.

Printed Baudelaire onto the face of his clock—after having broken off its hands.

There is always more time than you anticipate.

Said Malcolm Lowry. For whom there wasn't.

I was much further out than you thought
And not waving but drowning.

—Yis-ga-dal v'yis-ka-dash sh'may rab-bo.

I too have written some good books.

Said Nietzsche, overhearing someone's reference to literature in a fleeting moment's lucidity during his final madness.

Having died they are not dead.

Wrote Simonides of the Spartans slain at Plataea.

Keats, in a last letter some weeks before the end, telling a friend it is difficult to say goodbye:

I always made an awkward bow.

Tiny drops of water will hollow out a rock.

Lucretius wrote.

Als ick kan. Which Novelist finds himself several times repeating, even while not even sure in what language—is it six-hundred-year-old Flemish? And uncertain as to why he is caught up by van Eyck's use of it. That's it, I can do no more? All I have left? I can go no further?

Als ick kan?

Mankind which began in a cave and behind a windbreak will end in the disease-soaked ruins of a slum.

Said H.G. Wells.

The world began without man, and it will end without him.

Said Lévi-Strauss.

Swiftly the years, beyond recall.
Solemn the stillness of this spring morning.

—Reads the Arthur Waley translation of a Chinese fragment.

One man is born; another dies.

Being Euripides.

After death, nothing is.

Being Seneca.

The old man who will not laugh is a fool.

Said Santayana.

When Grandpa dies and his ashes are dropped into the ocean, may I have just a little bit of them? To put into something nice, so I can keep Grandpa with me for all time?

Pulvis et umbra sumus.

Quoth Horace. We are but dust and a shadow.

Dispraised, infirm, unfriended age.

Sophocles calls it.

Unregarded age in corners thrown.

Shakespeare echoes.

The worn copy of Donne's verses, inked throughout with notes in Coleridge's handwriting. And at the rear:

I shall die soon, my dear Charles Lamb, and then you will not be sorry that I bescribbled your book.

I am weary, Ananda, and wish to lie down.

Bhartrihari, fully fourteen hundred years ago, bemoaning the poverty of poets—in Sanskrit.

Then come kiss me, sweet-and-twenty,
Youth's a stuff will not endure.

Be patient now, my soul, thou hast endured worse than this.

Odysseus once says.

Mais où sont les neiges d'antan?

Is it true then, what they say—that we become stars in the sky when we die?

Asks someone in Aristophanes.

Access to Roof for Emergency Only.

Alarm Will Sound if Door Opened.

Old. Tired. Sick. Alone. Broke.

The old man who will not laugh is a fool.

Als ick kan.

Books For ALL Kinds of Readers

At ReadHowYouWant we understand that one size does not fit all types of readers. Our innovative, patent pending technology allows us to design new formats to make reading easier and more enjoyable for you. This helps improve your speed of reading and your comprehension. Our EasyRead printed books have been optimized to improve word recognition, ease eye tracking by adjusting word and line spacing as well as minimizing hyphenation. Our EasyRead SuperLarge editions have been developed to make reading easier and more accessible for vision-impaired readers. We offer Braille and DAISY formats of our books and all popular E-Book formats.

We are continually introducing new formats based upon research and reader preferences. Visit our web-site to see all of our formats and learn how you can Personalize our books for yourself or as gifts. Sign up to Become A **RHYW** Registered Reader.

www.readhowyouwant.com